NIGHTFALL

THE HUNTSMAN CLAN BOOK ONE

ROSE ALEXANDER

Cover: Black Glitter Press

Editing: Muddy Waters Editing

❀ Created with Vellum

DEDICATION

I dedicate this book to all the bratty kids who keep asking me to write a book they can read. You know who you are, and I love you all dearly.

PROLOGUE

A woman wearing a dark red cloak hurries down the empty street. It's just past midnight, and she's carrying a wicker basket covered with a light pink blanket, holding it close to her body, trying not to disturb the contents within. It's a cool spring night, the daytime not warm enough to take away the chill of the night. She stops on the steps of the orphanage and bangs on the door. An old woman groggily answers the door.

"Please take my baby. I can't keep her safe," the cloaked woman pleads with a quivering voice and tears shimmering in her eyes.

"What is she?" the old woman asks, squinting, confused, and half-asleep.

"She's a bear shifter."

"Let me have her then," the old woman replies with a sigh, holding out her arms for the baby.

The cloaked woman hands her over then rushes off into the night without another word.

CHAPTER ONE

"Amelia! It's time to go!" Mom shouts up the stairs.

"Coming Mom!" I holler back, bursting with energy.

I'm so excited, today is my sixteenth birthday. That means, as a bear shifter, I get to join my clan for my first shift. Examining in the mirror one, I love how nicely my ceremonial robes fall around my body. Then my eyes reach my face. There's nothing there that resembles my family. While I have light blonde hair that's wavy and almost to my butt, with dark brown, almost black eyes they all have chestnut brown hair and amber eyes. The button nose is so different from their long roman ones. Sighing, I turn away from the mirror. I've always felt different... like I don't quite belong. While my family is into music and academics, I've enjoyed sports and staying active. Just minor things that we don't have in common.

My parents treat me and my little brother, Josh, equally, so I don't know why I feel like I don't belong sometimes.

"I said hurry up," Mom calls up the stairs, her tone rising in pitch with her frustration.

I come running down the steps, with my cellphone in hand. My mom plucks it out of my grasp before I even notice what happened.

"That's not fair! I wanted to text Amanda and Tess before we got there," I pout, crossing my arms across my chest.

"You'll see both of them there, sweetie; they've already had their first runs," Mom reminds me, stroking my cheek.

"I know; I'm just excited. I can't wait to see what my bear looks like," I sigh, pulling away from her touch.

"She will be beautiful just like you." She kisses my forehead then swats my backside. "Now scoot."

I follow her to the car where my dad is already waiting. My brother watches from his bedroom window, sulking. I remember feeling that way a month ago when the first of my friends turned sixteen. It felt like time was dragging until today. He has two years to go yet. It makes me glad I'm the older sibling.

I'm a ball of nervous energy. My leg won't quit bouncing up and down. It feels like my skin is too tight. I can feel my bear under the surface, begging to come out.

"Settle down back there." My dad waggles his eyebrows.

"You know she won't until she shifts. Her bear is waking up." My mom chastises, lightly smacking his shoulder.

"I can't wait. Will it hurt when the alpha forces my bear out?" I chew on my bottom lip.

"Everyone has a different answer. I don't remember it hurting at all." Dad smiles proudly in the review mirror, while my mom snickers behind her hand. He glances out the corner of his eyes at her. What?"

"You complained for a week after your first shift." She reminds him, chuckling to herself.

"Don't scare our girl. She's exaggerating." He winks in the mirror.

"Don't worry, sweetie, it'll be great." Mom pivots in her seat, giving me a reassuring smile.

My skin tingles as we pull down the wooded drive to the clan building. It's nestled in the middle of the woods a few miles outside of town to help us stay hidden from humans and give us a place to let our bears run free. From the outside, it appears to be a boring, nondescript concrete building. The real magic happens when you step inside. As the center of our clan, there are rooms appointed to about anything you can think of. There are rec rooms for the kids and teenagers, classrooms for shifter studies, and a humongous gathering room where we share meals and special occasions. It's like a huge extended family.

I can feel my bear prowling under the surface, pacing back and forth. She grows more restless with each second that ticks by. By the time we enter the building, I feel like I'm bursting from the inside out.

The more shifters I'm around, the more restless my bear becomes. My nerves are frayed. If I don't shift soon, I don't know what is going to happen. I just need to shed my skin and run. Over the past week, I've began to feel her. It started as the whisper of a feeling, each day growing, until now she's buzzing right under the surface.

The enormous meeting room is full of long tables for the clan to eat together and congregate. At the end of the room, the alpha is standing on a raised stage. It's reserved for ceremonies and special occasions like a cubs first shift. After tonight, I won't be a cub anymore… I'll be a full member of the clan. My eyes widen as the reality sets in.

Out of the corner of my eye, I spy Amanda and Tess running towards me. A smile stretches across my face as I take off to meet them halfway.

"I can't believe you're finally here!" Amanda wraps her arms around me, excitement shining through her hazel eyes.

"This will be epic." Tess grins, her smile almost reaching both ears.

A man clears his throat behind me. I swivel around and see the alpha has walked up while we were talking. I drop my eyes in submission, not wanting to challenge his dominance. The alpha is a large man, built of solid muscle. He's nearly seven feet tall with jet black hair and a full, neatly trimmed beard. I would feel sorry for anyone who messed with him.

"Join me on stage now, Amelia." He orders, his glowing amber eyes pinning me to the spot.

"Yes, alpha." I glance up then immediately fix my eyes to the floor in front of him. Today would not be the right day to provoke a dominance battle.

I follow him on the stage, my bear even more restless in his presence.

"Well met clan members. Well met," the alpha booms, joy ringing through his voice.

"Well met alpha," the crowd roars in unison.

"Tonight, another shifter joins our ranks. Let's wish Amelia a happy birthday and join her on her first shift." The alpha gestures towards me and I give a small wave. "Let us convene outside to teach our newest bear how to run with the sleuth."

He strides across the room to a set of double doors large enough to allow full-grown grizzlies through. As a child, these doors always seemed so large and intimidating. Now, they are welcoming… a symbol of what's to come. I smile as I follow the alpha through the threshold into the sticky late summer warmth. The sun has set, but torches light the pathway to an outdoor amphitheater.

I ascend the stairs of the wooden platform in the center. *How many plays did we put on here as kids?* My mind flashes back to scene of my friends and me pretending to be wolf shifters, then another when we were in a Thanksgiving play.

I have so many good memories of this place. A smile spreads across my face as I realize it's about to be one more.

The crowd cheers as they fill the seats; my friends and family shouting the loudest. It's time for the ceremony to start. Last week my parents and I sat down with the alpha while we explained exactly what would happen tonight. All I must do is breathe and let him draw out my bear. The rest will take care of itself.

Taking a deep breath, I step forward and remove my robe, so I don't destroy it during the shift. Shifters aren't bothered by nudity as humans are. It's just a normal part of life for us. I learned in the locker rooms at school that humans try to cover themselves as much as possible. I still don't understand what the big deal is.

I stand in front of the crowd, nervous about the alpha forcing my first shift, but also excited. The pressure builds inside of me, like I could explode. The alpha stalks towards me, not saying a word. A guttural growl escapes his throats and my eyes dart up to meet his. The pressure intensifies, like an itch you can't scratch. It's not quite painful, but not comfortable either.

"Shift!" His voice rings out over the now silent amphitheater.

Suddenly, I burst, and the pressure dissipates. Wait a second… That isn't how this was supposed to go. I didn't feel any stretching, or my bones shifting, but the world appears different. The dark night is brighter as if I have night vision, and I'm no longer standing on two legs but down on all fours. The crowd gasps then goes silent. As my head swivels around to find what caused their reaction, I realize I'm way lower to the ground than I should be.

My paw catches my eye. My black, feline paw! Wait! *No... no... this can't be happening.* I'm a bear. I've seen my parents shift. Panic sets in and my breath comes out in fast huffs.

My mind is racing; how can I be a cat instead of a bear? I begin pacing across the stage, my muscles are moving in strange ways that feel foreign and familiar at the same time. My tail swishes and I jump. The crowd screams, which causes my panic to heighten.

"Calm sister, it's me Kylah, your panther spirit. I don't know how you ever thought we were a bear," my panther speaks in my head.

"But they raised me to be a bear," I mentally sob, heartbroken that my family lied.

"We are so much more than a bear, calm sister," Kylah purrs.

"How can this be? I don't want to be a panther." I sniff. My entire world is turning upside down and I don't know how to handle this.

"If the grass wanted to be blue would that change its color? We are what we are; you can't change that. I'll be here waiting for you to accept that," she huffs.

I need to get out of here. This amphitheater is too restrictive. I need freedom. I start to run but the alpha steps in front of me, and I slide forward as I scramble to stop.

"I'm sorry, little cub." His eyes fill with pain. "Shift!"

A wave of power washes over me and a wave of agonizing pain washes over me. My bones break apart then knit back together as the muscles rip and reshape themselves. I open my mouth to scream, but it comes out the yowl of a cat. Time loses all meaning as my body continues to torture me.

Finally, it stops. I lie on the ground sobbing, everything inch of my body is screaming in pain. Why was it so effortless when I shifted into my cat, but so excruciating to be called back to human?

"Considering recent developments, I'm canceling the run. There will be an emergency meeting of the elders now," the alpha orders. He turns to me and speaks softly. "I'm sorry I had to force you back. I know that was painful, but we couldn't risk your panther panicking and attacking someone."

"Ok," I sob, still trying to recover from the forced shift back.

"I wasn't panicking. That was all you, sister." Kylah rolls her eyes before laying down in the back of my mind.

I'm so confused right now; no one will look at me, not even my friends or parents. I crawl slowly over to my robe to put it back on.

My achy muscles finally obey, and I'm covered up. I glance around and the clearing has emptied of everyone but my parents. My mom is sobbing on my dad's shoulder and his face is in anguish. Now that my head is clearing, I finish putting the pieces together. I'm adopted, and they never told me. I'm so angry I want to scream. How could they do that to me?

"How could you?" I scream, angry tears streaming down my face.

"They assured us you were a bear shifter. When you were left at the orphanage, they talked to your birth mother," my mom sobs louder.

"Do I look like a bear now? The joke's on you then," I snarl then run out of the clearing.

I don't know where I'm going, except away from my parents. It's too far to run home, not that I want to see that place right now. The adrenaline leaves my body as I hit the clan building. I collapse against the wall in a heap and sob.

I can't believe no one told me. The signs were all there, but I never questioned them. This explains why I always felt different. Tears fall from my eyes as I contemplate my existence. Who am I now? Who were my birth parents? Why didn't they want me?

So many questions that I might never get the answers to. My sobs become whimpers, then they to die out until I'm just numb. I don't know how I should feel, so feeling nothing sounds like a good thing right now. I close my eyes and lean my head back against the wall and try to meditate for a while when I feel someone sit down next to me.

I growl then open my eyes and see the alpha. I freeze, scared of what will happen to me next.

"Relax, I'm just here to talk. You've been through a lot tonight, and I thought maybe you would need a shoulder to lean on," he mummers.

"I'm not in trouble?" I stammer. I'm not even a bear, so technically I've invaded their territory. Whether I knew it or not.

"Why would you be in trouble for being yourself?" His brow furrows.

"Are my parents in trouble then?" I bite my lip. Part of me wants the answer to be yes because I'm hurt... but that doesn't seem fair.

"They did nothing wrong but love you." He cocks his head and studies me.

"How can this happen? I grew up thinking I was a bear, and now, I'm a panther." I stare just below his eyes.

"You're not just a panther." He shakes his head.

"Because the only black panthers are royals," I mumble, my stomach in my throat.

That Huntsman clan are the rulers of all the shifters. It's the only clan that contains black panthers. I swallow down the lump forming in my throat, my stomach threatening to empty itself.

"Exactly." He grimaces.

"What will happen now?" My lower lip trembles. This is the worst situation I could imagine.

"I don't know. We have to contact the Huntsman clan and see what they say." He sighs, placing a large hand on my shoulder.

Kylah's ears perk up, her tail slowly swishing as she listens to the alpha.

"They won't hurt me, will they?" I ask, my heart beating faster. I take slow deep breathes, trying to quell the overwhelming urge to start running and never stop.

"We won't let them hurt you, little cub. You're still clan even if you look different," he replies, putting his log of an arm around my shoulders, giving me a squeeze. "Now, go apologize to your parents. Their only crime was loving you too much."

"Yes alpha," I mutter, getting up slowly.

I'm not ready to face them yet, but an order from the alpha is absolute. Plodding back to the clearing, I think of what to say to my parents.

Should I ask them why they didn't tell me I was adopted? Then it hit me; they didn't want me to think they loved me less. Now, I feel guilty for the way I acted, almost… them not telling me is why we are all so surprised. As an adopted shifter, I could have been anything.

I step into the clearing and find my parents sitting on one of the wooden benches. Their shoulders are slumped in defeat, and they appear to have aged. This isn't only affecting me.

"I'm sorry for yelling," I say, feeling ashamed.

"You had every right to yell," my dad sighs, anguish dulling his amber eyes. "We should have told you before today, just in case the orphanage was wrong."

"You've always been ours. We adopted you when you were just a baby. We didn't think it would matter." My mom wrings her hands together in her lap.

"I'm confused and scared," I whisper, hating how weak I sound. "My panther knows this isn't us, but I still feel like I'm supposed to be like you."

Mom stands up and wraps her arms around me. I lean

into her and cry for what I've lost… for what I've never had. My heart is breaking for a family I never knew, and for the one I thought I had.

"The alpha says I'm still clan, but what if they try to take me?" I chew on my bottom lip.

"We should be with other cats." Kylah yawns, uninterested in my feelings.

"We'll cross that bridge when we get there." My dad's face bunches up in anguish.

"Let's go home," Mom decides, looking tired and defeated.

The ride back to the house seems to take forever. I can't stop thinking about the what-ifs. What if no one accepts me now that I'm not a bear? What if I'm forced to leave? What if the Huntsman clan wants me punished for existing? I've never heard of a panther existing outside of their clan, so I have no idea what they'll do.

"Hello?" my mom answers her phone.

"I understand," she replies to whomever she's speaking to. "How soon?"

"I understand, alpha, goodbye." She ends the call.

"What was that about?" I watch her expectantly.

"We'll talk about it when we get home." Her shoulders slump.

I stay quiet, not wanting to add to her misery. Staring out the window, the world appears strange and foreign. Even in my human form, I see better in the dark since I shifted. We arrive back at the house, and I'm ready to speak with my parents, but they take off to their bedroom, not allowing me the opportunity. I grab my cell phone off the table where my mom left it and run up the stairs to my room. I find Amanda's name and hit call.

"Lia, I'm not allowed to talk to you. My parents won't let me," Amanda whispers, guilt tinging her voice.

"But the alpha said I'm still clan," I gasp, hurt that she is turning her back on me.

"I'm sorry, Lia. My parents want nothing to do with a Huntsman," she whispers back then hangs up.

My stomach drops. Amanda and I have been best friends since we were in diapers. I can't believe her parents would shun me like that. My fingers shake as I dial Tess's number. I debated texting her, but I'm afraid she won't answer.

"Lia, you can't call again. You're not one of us," she hisses then hangs up.

I didn't even say hello. Tears burn my eyes as I crawl on my bed. What was supposed to be a happy occasion has turned into the worst day of my life. I hug my pillow and cry myself to sleep.

CHAPTER TWO

"Wake up." Mom gently shakes my shoulder.

"Tomorrow," I pout then roll over and put the pillow over my head.

"We need to talk." She pulls the pillow off my face, leaving no room for argument.

I sit up, still in the robe from my ceremony, my hair a tangled mess.

"You can get cleaned up then meet us downstairs for a family meeting." She lays the pillow back on the bed.

She leaves the room, closing the door behind her. I crawl out of bed, pull on a pair of yoga pants and a loose t-shirt then run a brush through my hair.

The events from the prior night play on a loop in my head, bringing back the crushing pain. I'm not who I thought I was. I don't belong here, and I don't belong with The Huntsman. I just want to go back to sleep and have this all be a bad dream. I should be a bear.

"You need to accept that I am you and you are me," Kylah says, stretching from the back of my mind.

"I don't want to accept that I am a panther." I take a deep

breath, attempting to keep my emotions in check.

"It's who we are. We may share a body, but we also share emotions, desires, well pretty much everything. You will see in time," she says before laying back down.

I ignore her. Everything that happened the night before replays through my mind like a nightmare I can't wake up from. How did I never realize the animal inside of me wasn't a bear? Twenty-four hours ago, I was on the verge of a life-changing event, one that was supposed to be joyous and exciting. But instead, I watched everything I ever thought to be true implode in front of me in an instant. Today, I get to deal with the fallout of that implosion. I take a deep breath then go down to the family room to face the truth.

"Why did I have to get up early?" Josh grumbles as he stomps down the stairs.

"This affects all of us, so you need to know what happened last night." Dad runs his hands down his face. His eyes have lost their jovial glimmer I've grown accustomed to.

"He doesn't know yet?" My head whips back and forth between my parents and Josh.

"We went to bed when we got home." Mom refuses to meet my eyes.

"I received a call from the alpha this morning. There will be a representative from the Huntsman clan visiting today." Dad picks at the skin on his thumb.

"Why?" Fear flashes across his face. The Huntsman are the enforcers… typically, they only venture this way if they are punishing a shifter for revealing our secrets.

"Because I'm not a bear shifter; I'm a black panther!" I growl. Kylah stretches then prowls closer to the surface.

"Very funny, Lia." He rolls his eyes. "But why are they really coming?"

"Because I was adopted, but no one told us. When I

shifted last night, I was a panther and not a bear. Now everything is messed up." I glare at him.

"How cool is that! Your part of the royal family?" His eyes widen in awe.

"See the boy understands what we are." Kylah swishes her tail.

"Not cool at all," I grumble.

"Now children, focus," my mom chides.

"What can we expect?" I begin pacing across the room.

"I don't really know. They could leave the whole thing alone, or..." Mom trails off.

"Or what?" I stop pacing and stare at her, my heart pounding in my chest. We've all heard stories of shifters disappearing with the enforcers, never to be seen again.

"Or they could force you to return with them. It's within their rights," my dad finishes, his face flushing to a deep crimson.

"I won't go. They can't make me!" I scream.

My heart starts pounding, faster and faster as my chest begins to seize. Suddenly, it becomes more difficult to breathe and my skin tingles. I can't stay here. They can't take me if they can't find me.

"Amelia, wait!" my mom shouts, her voice fading out behind me. "Somebody go after her!"

I don't listen. I'm unable to think, only heed the urge to run as far and fast as I can. I pass through the threshold and my bare feet pound the pavement in a steady rhythm. The world passes by, blurred by my racing mind. The pavement turns to gravel and I move to the grass, unable to slow down, lest the emotions I'm running from catch up to me. Kylah paces back and forth, her tail swishing in annoyance. I can feel her need to run and who am I to deny my other half?

"Do it." I slow to a stop and lean my hand on my knees to catch my breath.

"Thank you, sister," she purrs.

Pressure builds as I watch her running towards the surface in my mind's eye. Suddenly, it explodes, my clothes ripping away in the process. As soon as our feet hit the ground, I hand her the reins.

She propels us forward, our muscles bunching and releasing as we glide across the forest floor. The wind whips across our face, causing our whiskers to vibrate.

My senses are overwhelmed by all the new information. Sounds are more pronounced as small creatures scurry under the ground covering. As we slow, I open my mouth and am met with an explosion of new smells. It's like nothing I can describe. It's as if it's taken on a new dimension. Instead of smelling just my surroundings, I can scent the field mice burrowed next to a nearby tree. I smell squirrels in the tree above me, and a wolf who's claimed this territory as his own. All of this above what I would normally sense with my human nose.

We stretch out our muscles, and Kylah takes us into a nearby tree, using her claws to quickly climb to a branch she finds suitable. We lay down and she closes her eyes, tail flicking in the air to the side.

I startle awake. I grab ahold of the branch underneath me, terrified of falling. A scream escapes my throat as my balance falters.

"Amelia, where are you?" A deep voice floats up to my ears.

"Amelia, come home," my mom sobs.

"I'm up here!" I yell back, as I slip. Now I'm dangling above the ground, holding onto the limb above my head for dear life.

The alpha reaches the base of the tree first.

"Up here." I grunt, trying to will my hands to hold on.

"Your panther took over," he chuckles, his eyes alight with

amusement. "At least you took off away from people. Let go, and I'll catch you."

Is he crazy? But it's not like I have many options. Taking a deep breath, I close my eyes and let go, falling into the alpha's arms. Good thing he has great depth perception. Hitting the ground would have been painful.

My mom runs forward just as he sets me on the ground. She's carrying a black terry cloth robe and hands it to me. I quickly slip it on, covering my bare body.

"We were so worried about you." She wraps her arms around me, tears flowing freely down her cheeks.

"I'm sorry; I didn't know what to do." I hang my head.

"Yes, you did. That's why we ran," Kylah huffs, unimpressed.

"You did the right thing. A panther stuck in a house is a dangerous thing," my dad explains. "We just didn't know how far you would go before we could catch you."

"How do you get used to hearing a voice only you can hear?" I ask, confused why no one ever said anything about their bear speaking.

"What do you mean?" Mom's eyes are filled with concern.

"Kylah talks a lot; I guess I just assumed your bear did too," I sigh, feeling even more different.

"No, my bear doesn't have a name, and she is more of a feeling that her own presence. If we would have known you were a panther, we would have learned more about them for you," Mom answers gently, guilt marring her amber eyes. "Did your panther tell you her name was Kylah?"

"Yes, that's why I thought your animal spoke to you." I bite my lip, trying to stifle the tears that threaten to fall.

"We can ask the representative the Huntsman clan sent." She pats my hand.

"Where am I?" I survey my surroundings. Now that I'm alert, I don't recognize this forest at all.

"You ran about thirty miles." The alpha chuckles,

glancing up at the tree covered sky. "The Huntsman representative is waiting back at the clan building so we better head back."

"Do I have to go meet with him today? This is all happening so fast." My body begins to tremble. I take slow deep breathes, fighting the urge to run again.

"You do, but we'll face this together." Mom nods her head as her eyes harden in resolve. "He might have answers we don't."

"The car is on the road about half a mile that way." The alpha points to the east.

"I'm sorry I caused so much trouble." I stare down at my feet.

"This is nothing compared to other messes I've cleaned up. Come on cub, time to face the music." He bumps me gently with his huge frame.

I follow the others in silence, scared of what will happen once we reach the clan building. I mull over what I do know about The Huntsman clan. It's made up of the big cat races. There are always four queens. The lion, the tiger, the panther, and the leopard. There are lesser cats that belong to the clan, but all black panthers literally descend from royalty and are nobility.

"Why would a noble give up their baby and lie about what kind of shifter they were? I mean, they knew when I turned sixteen the truth would come out," I wonder aloud.

"To keep us alive," Kylah whispers.

"Maybe they hid the pregnancy because they were young. I'm sure the orphanage wouldn't have taken you if they had known you were a black panther," Mom tries to answer my question.

"It still doesn't make sense. Now we're all dealing with the mess because of a little lie," I sigh. Is ignorance bliss or is the truth just wasted on me?

"You're the same as we've always been," Kylah flicks her tail in annoyance.

"I'm glad they lied. I love being your mom," Mom whispers, her voice trembling.

"I love that you're my mom too." I stop and glance over at her. "I'm sorry if I sound ungrateful, but this has all been confusing. I don't know who I am anymore. It's not that I don't want to be your daughter… I just feel lost."

"I know, sweetie. You're taking this better than I would have." She rubs her arms to keep her hands busy as we continue moving.

I wish I had someone my own age to talk to but that doesn't seem likely anytime soon. My heart aches at the thought.

"Amanda and Tess said their parents won't let them talk to me anymore," I blurt out, tearing up at the loss.

"We don't need bears anyway," Kylah snarls, agitated that I'm upset.

"I'll have a word with them," The alpha's eyes grow dark. "We don't turn our backs on clan, ever."

"I don't want anyone getting in trouble over me." I regret saying anything. Getting them in trouble won't help my cause.

"Little cub, only their own actions can cause repercussions. You didn't tell them to treat you differently. That's their own bias they are trying to pawn off on you." His voice is firm, but kind.

"Still, I feel like I'm tattling," I admit, staring down at my feet.

"I'll talk to the clan." He rests a hand on my shoulder.

"Why are you being so nice to me?" I stop in my tracks and examine him.

"I'm adopted too, so I get what you're going through.

Only, I grew up with wolves." He winks and drops the conversation.

My jaw drops and I stand there baffled. I would have never guessed he would have grown up with anyone but bears. How difficult would that have been for him? Finding out he was not a wolf and no one understanding what he was going through? I'm lucky to have him here for me. I wonder how he ended up with bears, but I'm afraid to ask. The group keeps moving forward and I jog to catch up.

We make it to the car, and I climb in the backseat between my parents. Mom grabs my hand in hers, absently patting it. Dad's arm is around my back, rubbing the arm farthest from his. Their actions have me even more worried than I was before. I can't help but think they know something I don't. I take deep breaths, trying to calm myself as Kylah prowls just beneath the surface.

"We should just run. I don't enjoy being cooped up," she growls.

"Kylah wants to run." My heart pounds in my chest. What would happen if I shifted right here?

"Don't worry little cub; she can't come out unless I allow it." The alpha sets my mind to rest.

"Thank you," I whisper, even though I'm not totally convinced.

We ride the rest of the way in silence. My mind is running wild, imagining the worst-case scenarios. I can't imagine life away from my parents or my clan. The Huntsman clan is such a mystery.

We pull up to the clan building way too soon for my liking. My dad gets out, and I reluctantly follow him. I drag behind as we make our way to the building. Each step feels like it's taking me closer to my doom. Maybe this won't be so bad? He might take one look at me and leave laughing. What kind of cat shifter would I make since I was raised by bears?

We enter the building and take a right. The polished wood floor is cold and smooth under my bare feet as the alpha stops in front of the meeting room. I step inside and my eyes fall on a tall, thin man sitting at the long, oak conference table in a black suit with a white shirt, and tiffany blue tie. His hair is a golden blonde and he has a day's growth of facial hair. My eyes meet his, seeing my own black eyes mirrored back to me.

"He's a leopard." Kylah sniffs the air.

"Amelia, I presume?" He smiles; his entire face lighting up. "I hope you enjoyed your run?"

"Yes, sir," I stutter. He appears kind, but that scares me even more. I don't want to like that man that is deciding my fate.

"He's good; we should like him," Kylah purrs.

"Relax, Amelia. This isn't an interrogation. We're just trying to understand how one of our own ended up here. My name is Jack LeDonne." He stands up and offers his hand for me to shake, flashing me a lopsided smile.

"Isn't it obvious? My birth mother gave me up and my real mom adopted me," I snark then cover my mouth. *Did I just speak to him like that? What is getting into me?*

Jack laughs; his entire body shaking. "She's definitely one of ours."

"You can be nicer to Jack, child," I hear a male voice in my head.

"Who are you?" I ask mentally. Maybe this all just a fevered dream, or I've gone completely mad. I'm hearing multiple voices now.

"I am Jace, Jack's leopard," he purrs smoothly, Kylah purring back.

"I'm sorry; I didn't mean to be rude. My mom raised me better than that," I apologize aloud to Jack. Did his leopard really just speak in my head? I'm so confused by everything going on.

"It's perfectly ok. You've had a rough couple of days." He winks, giving a small grin. "I need you to shift now please."

"I don't want to." I shake my head, not wanting to show him Kylah.

"Since she refused, alpha, can you please force her shift?" Jack shifts his eyes down, his face falling.

"Jack says sorry, Amelia," Jace whispers.

"Sorry cub," Alpha says with sad eyes.

"I'll shift!" My eyes widen, remembering the pain from last night when the alpha forced me back to my human form.

I take the robe off and take a deep breath feeling my panther prowling at the surface. The pressure intensifies, and then I explode into panther form.

"She's a direct descendant of the royal line." Jack gasps, eyes wide in shock. "This changes everything!"

"Please don't be upset," Jace says anxiously.

"How can you tell?" My mom rubbing her arms as if she's cold.

"See the lack of white on her body? Only the royal line lacks those markings. I must report my findings immediately. Excuse me for a moment." He rushes out of the room, glancing behind him one last time before he's out of sight.

"Little cub, focus on your human form. I don't want to force you back again," the alpha coaxes.

I do as he says and visualize my body as if I was looking in the mirror. I can feel my bones and muscles shifting, but it's painless like when I've shifted into my panther. I'm panting, kneeling on my knees when the transformation is complete. I breathe a sigh of relief as I take the robe back from my mom.

"Why do I explode out to my animal form, but it's slow to

turn back?" I put my arms through the robe and tie it around my waist.

"I'm too strong for how young we are," Kylah states her thought as if I should know.

"We need to teach you control. Kylah shouldn't be in charge," Jace comments.

"Mind your own business leopard," Kylah huffs.

"Not sure, most shifters shift the same going either direction," the alpha answers.

"Maybe that Jack guy will know." My dad tries to be optimistic.

"Maybe, but I'm nervous of his reaction," Mom rubs her hands together.

"Don't jump to conclusions," the alpha barks, glaring at my parents as if they've done something wrong.

"Kylah says it's because she's too strong for my age," I answer my own question aloud.

"That's so interesting you can hear your animal." My mom's eyes widen in awe.

"What happened to you when your clan found you were a bear instead of a wolf?" I finally work up the nerve to ask the alpha. I become hopeful he'll tell me everything will be all right.

"They moved me to a bear clan," he answers quietly.

"Be honest. They will take me, won't they?" My chest tightens.

"We should go with them," Kylah says, confused as to why I want to be with bears.

"They probably will, little cub. After that reaction, I don't think I can stop them." His voice quivering, betraying his emotions.

"At least my cat will be happy about it." I huff, crossing my arms across my chest. My eyes burn as I fight the tears that are trying to force their way out. I'm tired of crying. I would rather be mad.

My mom covers her mouth as tears flow down her cheeks, leaning into my dad for support. He holds her tight while his eyes dull with pain. I can't even comfort them because I feel the same. I plop on the floor, bury my head in my hands, and stop fighting the tears. I will never belong anywhere now. This is supposed to be my home, but I don't belong anymore. and, if he takes me, it won't ever be home again. But The Huntsman clan can't be home either. I've never even met another cat before today.

I hear the door open and close, but I don't bother glancing up. I can smell that it's Jack before he approaches. My senses in this form are improving already.

"You have to come with us, please understand," Jace explains in my head.

"I've talked to the four queens. They want the girl to integrate back into the Huntsman clan, effective immediately," Jack explains, a sad note in his voice.

I refuse to acknowledge his presence. If I ignore him, maybe he'll go away and leave us alone. I feel a large hand on my shoulder and raise my head. The alpha's expression leaves no room for argument. Years of conditioning make it so I must obey, even though it's the worst thing that could ever happen.

"Do I at least get to go home and grab my stuff?" I whisper, scared my voice will betray me.

"No need. We'll buy you more appropriate attire on the way." He stands next to the door.

"I'm not leaving here in a robe," I wail, unable to keep it together. "I need a goodbye with my family."

"Fine, we'll go to your house so you can get dressed, but that's it. One outfit." His eyes betraying his sadness.

"He doesn't want to take you, but we don't want to die," Jace says then leaves.

"Why would you die?" I ask, feeling confused, but I'm met with silence.

We follow Jack into his limo and ride in silence to my house. I don't know what to say, and my emotions are churning. I oscillate between tears burning my eyes and rage building in my chest so intensely I worry it will force me to shift. When we pull to a stop at the curb, I run inside. Taking the stairs two at a time, I find Josh in the hallway and wrap my arms around him in a tight hug.

"What's wrong with you?" He pats my back awkwardly.

"They're taking me away. They only let me come home to get dressed then I have to go." My voice gets caught in my throat as a sob escapes.

"Taking you where?" He pulls me back and examines my face. "Mom? Dad? What's happening with Lia?"

I pull out of his arms and rush into my bedroom as my chest grows so tight, I think my heart could stop beating.

I put on a pair of yoga plants, a plain black tee, and my favorite running shoes then go back downstairs after one last survey of my room I'm leaving behind.

"It's a new beginning." Kylah tries to comfort me.

As I turn the corner into the living room, my parents and Josh are talking in hushed whispers that stop when my mom notices my presence.

"I don't want to leave you." I rush forward, throwing myself in my mom's arms.

"I know and we don't want you to leave either, but we don't have a choice. The only thing left is to make us proud and stay strong." She squeezes me tightly.

"We love you. Call us when you get settled in." My dad kisses my forehead, then his eyes dart to the doorway.

Jack leans against the doorframe, waiting for me to finish.

"There's really no way I can stay here?" I pivot out of my mom's embrace and stare at him, my eyes pleading him to reconsider.

"Amelia, if it were up to me…" He trails off as his eyes cloud over as if lost in a distant memory. "Come along, we must go."

He grabs my hand and pulls me behind him towards the door. I hate to admit it, but he feels familiar in a way he shouldn't. I glance back over my shoulder one last time and wish I hadn't. My mom is quietly sobbing on my dad's shoulder while Josh watches on, unable to help. Emotions suck, and I will not allow mine to make me weak. I square my jaw and will my own tears to stay put.

"Jack wants to help you; don't hate him," Jace says.

"I don't understand why she isn't happy to go to our real home," Kylah tells him.

"How do you get used to the voices in your head?" I grit my teeth.

"It's been that way since I first shifted. I always knew Jace would talk to me when he named himself. I'm sorry you weren't brought up with the knowledge." Jack refuses to meet my eyes.

$\mathcal{W}$e settle in the back of Jack's limo. An awkward silence hangs over us, making the air thick. I refuse to give him attention or engage in any further conversation, so we'll just have to deal with it. He destroyed my life in one phone call… Why couldn't he have just pretended I didn't exist?

"I'm really not your enemy, you know. I convinced the queens to allow you to integrate instead of killing you." He tries to catch my eye.

"Listen to him." Jace paces on the edge of my mind.

"What!" I examine his face. Why in the world would they want me dead?

"Queen Rani informed me they were split. Two wanted you dead and the other two said to integrate. I can't for the life of me figure out why they would want you dead. It's not like you pose a threat to anyone… and panthers are so rare." He runs his hand through his honey colored hair. "Anyway, you're my responsibility so let's make the best of this."

"Well, thank you for saving my life, but I have no idea what I'm walking into. Where will I stay? I don't have family there that I know of." I try to absorb the fact I nearly died just for existing. "How could they want me dead?

"The way our clan is set up, all children your age attend Nightfall Academy. It's a boarding school, so you will live there during the school year. I volunteered for you to live with me during breaks," he explains. "As for the why someone could want you dead… I suspect they are thinking of themselves. There is a prophecy that has been the catalyst to several panther princesses dying over the years. We can talk more about that later if you want."

"Yes, we want." Kylah perks up.

"Why would you do that?" I ask perplexed.

"I don't always agree with everything that is done. If you would have had even one white hair, I was prepared to leave you with your family. But given your linage… I couldn't do it," he sighs, staring at his hands again.

I have to assimilate into a new society… go to a new school… Oh no! What do they teach them there? Am I ever going to catch up with my peers?

"How am I supposed to catch up in school? The other kids have been learning this stuff their entire lives." I start hyperventilating.

"You're a smart girl. I can tell by the questions you're already asking. You'll catch up in no time. We have a few days to go over the basics before term starts." He tries to calm me.

"Stop worrying. I can't get out and run." Kylah paces back and forth, just under my skin.

"Let's talk about something else. I don't want to think right now. My life is upside down, and I just want to go home to my mom and dad." I sniff, trying not to cry. "Can we control when our cats talk to other people?"

"I wish we could. They don't always tell us what they tell other people." He gives me a sideways glance.

"What is that look about?" I put my hands on my hips.

"Our cats don't just talk to random people... Don't worry about it right now. Everything will make sense eventually." He shakes his head, a small smirk playing on his lips. "What type of clothes do you like? We have a budget of ten thousand dollars for everything you need."

"That's way more money than we need." My eyes widen.

"You'll need a laptop, a new cell phone, tablet, clothes for off school time, uniforms, and anything else you would like for entertainment. It'll add up quickly. The students at your school have certain standards. You need to dress the part and present yourself as your class." He chuckles.

"So, snobby rich kids." I roll my eyes.

"Exactly. You'll present yourself as rich and confident, even if you must fake it. They don't need to know your past." He glances over at me and grins.

"How will they not know already?" My forehead bunches together.

"They will know that you weren't raised here, but not about the adoption. There are cities all over the world where our kind are stationed to help police the other shifters." He fidgets with his hands in his lap. "Even with your lineage, there's a possibility you were raised in one such place."

"I'll do what I have to. It's not like I have a choice," I growl through gritted teeth, crossing my arms over my chest.

"We'll be happy soon, I can feel it," Kylah whispers.

"I'm happy you're here," Jace responds to her.

"There's the spirit." Jack rolls his eyes.

"Yeah, whatever," I sigh as I twist and gaze out the window. "Where's this clan located? No one has ever said."

"It's in Southern California, on an island that humans don't know about." A smile spreads across his face as he speaks.

"We're driving the entire way?" My eyes widen. This is going to be a long car ride.

"Of course not. We have to take a boat to the island." He winks, teasing me.

"How long will it take to get to California?" I ask.

"Well, once we get to the airport, we should be there by morning." He chuckles.

"He likes you so he's trying to distract you," Jace says.

I roll my eyes. I'm quiet until we get to the airport. It's a small one, not like the commercial lines. There's a private jet waiting, and the limo pulls up right next to it. The driver opens the door and I climb out after Jack. There's no luggage, so as soon as we board the plane, the limo drives off. Something about that simple act seals my fate. This is really happening and there's no going back. I settle into a large, cushioned seat and put on the seatbelt.

"The Huntsman clan does have some perks." Jack grins as he settles in next to me. "When we get to LA, we'll go shopping."

As much as I hate the situation that I'm in, I'm a teenage girl and shopping is exciting. Why can't I just stay mad? Guilt washes over me for anticipating this part of the trip. It's not that I want to be away from home, but it's happening anyways. Is it wrong for me to enjoy the perks? I need to put my best foot forward and accept what is happening since I can't change it

"Can I use your phone?" A wave of homesickness hits me, making my chest ache.

"Not while we're in the air. No cellphones on the plane." Jack grimaces. "You can, however, call them after we land. I'm sure they are eager to hear from you."

"I'm sure they are too." My eyes tear up and I swallow hard as I force them back.

He notices my discomfort and changes the subject. "Do you want to watch a movie?"

"Sure." I shrug.

Jack puts a movie on. I watch the opening credits play as the plane takes off. A man is standing at a train station complaining about Valentine's Day. As he boards the train, I drift off to sleep.

A digging sound causes my eyes to open. I glance around blurry eyed, not remembering where I am for a moment.

"It's just the seat belt sign. It's time to land." Jack points at the little light on the panel in front of us.

My stomach growls loudly. I haven't eaten all day, and with everything that's happened it never crossed my mind.

"We'll go get food as soon as we land." Jack grimaces. "It hadn't occurred to me you wouldn't have eaten."

"It's my fault." I blush.

"We all should have remembered to feed you before we left. You shifted twice in one day and you must be starving." He shakes his head.

The plane lands at a much larger airport than we took off from. Hundreds of people stand, milling around. Voices echo throughout the airport, yet I've never felt so alone. Everything I knew, everything I believed is now gone, and the unknown awaits me. We make our way towards a man holding a sign that reads Huntsman. Jack tells him where to go as we make our way to the waiting car.

We settle into the backseat then drive off. The landscape passing by is so different than my quiet little town. The cityscape stretches as far as the eye can see, with large looming buildings on the horizon. Besides an odd palm tree and lawn, it feels so devoid of life. I shake my head. I can't understand why anyone would choose to live this way.

"I figured you'd like to eat quickly," Jack explains as we pull up in front of a diner.

We go inside, and my stomach cramps as the smell of greasy food wafts towards us. We sit in a booth and wait for the waitress to bring us menus.

"Hi, my name is Mags. What can I get you to drink?" the waitress hands us plastic-coated menus.

"Water for me," I reply.

"Coffee," Jack says curtly.

"Creamer or sugar?" she asks.

"Black."

She excuses herself to go get our drinks. I can't decide on what to get. It's afternoon, but breakfast sounds amazing and thankfully, they serve it all day. The waffles sound fantastic, but so do the omelets. I'll order both. If Jack has a ten-thousand-dollar budget, he can afford two meals.

Mags returns with our drinks and takes a small notebook a pen out of her apron.

"What can I get you to eat?" She smiles.

"Can I get a ham and cheese omelet with sausage and bacon on the side, and the berry waffles?" I grin back at her.

"Give me what she's having." Jack waves her off, not even bothering to make eyes contact with the woman.

Mags collects our menus then walks off to put our order in, and I glare at Jack.

"Why are you being so rude?" I hiss, embarrassed to be with such a rude person.

"She's just a human." He shrugs wearing a puzzled expression.

"Why do you care about a human?" Jace asks.

"Now I know that I won't ever fit in with you." I narrow my eyes. "I was taught we treat others how we want to be treated."

"They can learn, don't give up," Kylah starts pacing.

"You're right. I'm embarrassed. My time at court has affected my attitude and thinking." His eyes widen then he glances at me. "I'll try and do better."

"Then be nice when she brings our food," I demand then

change the subject. "Can I use your phone to call my parents while we wait?"

"Of course." He hands me his phone.

I walk outside to make sure I can hear and dial my mom's cell number, my foot tapping as it rings.

"Hello?" she answers, her voice sounding tired.

"Hi Mommy," I choke out. All the emotions I've been feeling the past twenty-four hours swirling together.

"Amelia! Goddess, it's good to hear your voice!" Mom exclaims, relief and hurt both clear in her voice.

"You too," I sob, the full weight of what's happening hits me.

I thought hearing her voice would make me feel better, but instead it magnifies the pain of leaving. Why does the world have to be so messed up?

"Keep your head up and be brave. Don't show them any weakness. You are a strong, confident, young woman. I know it's hard, but just know we're always proud of you, and you'll always be our daughter." Her voice grows strong. I can feel her trying to hold it together for both of us.

"I'll try. I just miss you so much," I sniffle. "I don't know who I am or what I am anymore, but I'll be brave for you."

"We miss you too, but you have to play the hand life has dealt you." Her voice softens.

"Ok, I need to go eat. I just wanted to hear your voice. I love you," I say between sniffles and tears.

"Go eat. I love you too. We'll talk again soon." Mom ends the call.

They understand we need our new home, don't cry, Kylah says, brushing the back of my mind.

I stare at the phone for a minute, wipe my face the best I can, and head back inside to the booth. When I reach the table, Mags is arriving with the food. Once she has all the food on the table, I stare greedily at it.

"Can I get you anything else?" She smiles sweetly at Jack.

"No, thank you. This looks great." Jack grins.

"Thank you," I reply before I stuff the first bite of omelet in my mouth.

I shovel food in my mouth like I haven't eaten in weeks. I didn't realize how hungry I was until I started. I finish my food in record time and find that Jack has kept up with me. He flashes me a grin and waves Mags over for the check. He pays the check then we get back in the limo and drive off.

"Where are we going next?" I twirl my hair between two fingers.

"Shopping is next on the agenda. Clothes first then supplies." He winks.

"Where are we shopping at?" I hate that I'm getting so excited.

"Why do you care about clothes; they are just an inconvenience," Kylah huffs and lays down to nap.

"You'll see." He grins.

Time drags slowly as we crawl through the congested traffic on the fourteen-lane freeway. As the driver exits, we are in a busy shopping district. I press my face to the window, watching people rush about their business. We stop in front of car park, where the driver let's up out before pulling underground.

"Money will not go very far here," I whisper, my stomach rolling and tying itself in knots.

"It's fine. You'll get everything you need." Jack smiles, chuckling under his breath.

"Ok," I reply hesitantly, not wanting to get my hopes up.

My head swivels back and forth as we walk down the busy sidewalk. I've never seen so many people in the same place. I follow him into a shop like I've never seen before. A woman peers down her nose at us, her lip curled up in disgust.

I'm ready to turn around and leave when Jack pulls a black card out of his wallet.

"How can I help you today?" She rushes over to us, plastering a smile on her face.

"She needs a complete wardrobe." He raises his eyebrow. "Unless our money isn't good here?"

"Give us an hour, and she'll be good to go." Her smile reaches her eyes. I can almost see the dollar signs swimming behind them. "Follow me."

I take a deep breath and follow the haughty saleswoman up a set of stairs to a cream room with an oversized leather couch against the wall. This is not the kind of store or clothes I would have ever bought. I guess it's just another part of my identity I'm losing. It makes my chest hurt to think about, so I push it to the back of my mind. I need to be strong for my mom, if for nothing else. I need to be able to tell her I'm doing fine next time we talk.

"What's your style preferences?" She stares at me with that fake sugary sweet smile.

"We should eat her," Kylah growls.

"Huh?"

"What type of clothes do you normally wear?" She taps her foot, unable to hide the irritation from her voice.

"Just jeans and t-shirts mainly." I bite the inside of my cheek to keep from snapping.

She rolls her eye. "We have a lot of work to do then."

"Don't let her speak to you like that," Kylah nearly shouts while pacing under my skin.

"If you're going to talk to me like that, I'm sure we can find somewhere else to shop," I snap. I leave the room, slamming the door behind me then stomp down the stairs.

"What's wrong?" Jack checks me over when I come into view.

"That woman is horrible! I'm not shopping here," I reply through a clenched jaw.

"Kylah told him what happened," Jace whispers at the edge of my mind.

"Let's go, there are other stores." He clenches his teeth.

The saleswoman reaches the bottom of the stairs. "I didn't get to show you anything we have to offer."

"Then you should have treated her better. I will be calling the store owner. The Huntsman have been doing business here for years." Jack scowls at her.

Her face blanches to a pale white, and I secretly enjoy her discomfort as we leave the store. Jack leads me down the street, passing the next two storefronts before entering the third.

"Welcome, how can I help you?" The saleswoman smiles, her brown eyes radiating kindness.

"She needs a complete wardrobe; can you help her?" Jack raises eyebrow.

"Certainly, I'd love to. Can you come with me so we can see what you'd like?" she asks kindly, no fakery to her.

"This one is better," Kylah purrs, laying back down.

I smile nervously at Jack before following her. She isn't rubbing me the wrong way like the first lady. She leads me to a room with purple plush chairs. She motions for me to sit, then takes the other one.

"Do you have a particular style you like?" she asks, waiting patiently for my response.

"I just wear jeans and t-shirts, really. I've never shopped in a place like this," I admit, feeling awkward.

"That's ok. We have several different styles you can try. We'll find out what's a good fit for you." She smiles. "Are you opposed to trying skirts and dresses?"

"I can try anything. The worst that can happen is I say no." I shrug, chewing on my lip nervously.

"Great attitude! Now, I need to take your measurements," She stands up and claps her hands.

I push myself to my feet and stand awkwardly while she measures me every way you can measure a person. When she finishes, she announces she'll be back with clothes for me to try on.

I sit back down and try to picture what she'll bring back. Will it be simple street clothes that I could wear every day? Or, will she try to bring things like you see in the magazines? I laugh out loud picturing myself wearing a high fashion dress you see in the magazines. I might be in shape, but I'm no fashion model.

She returns with a rack of clothes with all kinds of styles on it. There's too much there for me to sort through immediately and my eyes widen. Does she want me to try on all these clothes?

"Ok, we need to find out what your personal style really is. Do you like the punk look, or the preppy look... or are you the princess type?" She holds up an example for each style.

"I like the punk look, if it doesn't go overboard," My shoulders loosen when I see the ripped jeans and casual t-shirt. "I like wearing black too."

"Ok, great! That makes this super easy for us! And fun." She winks. "Wait right here."

She pulls the rack behind her as she exits the room. I sit on my hands to keep from fidgeting. This is more uncomfortable that I had imagined. I used to love to shop, but that's when I got to peruse and pick out clothes I liked. This feels more like a test. One that I can't pass. At least this saleswoman is a sweetheart.

She steps through the doorway again, pulling a longer rack of clothes in with her.

"Have at it." She smiles, her eyes wrinkling at the edges. "If you see anything you want to try on, just grab it."

"Thank you." I grin and hop up to inspect the rack.

There are lots of black clothes, but all have pops of color added in somewhere. I grab an outfit and try it on. It fits perfectly, and I'm in love. I go out and look in the three-way mirror. The dark blue jeans hug my hips perfectly and the black t-shirt fits without being too baggy or tight. I grin at myself in the mirror then grab another outfit. Once I've finished, I'm excited about the wardrobe. I even picked some skirts and dresses.

"I've added bras and panties to match each outfit." The sales-clerk points out as she carries my selections to the register.

"Thank you." I grin, loving the thought of having a new style.

"Now, let's go get you checked out." She chuckles as she takes her place behind the register.

"I take it you had a better experience?" Jack raises an eyebrow.

"It was very nice." I grin back.

He chuckles as she rings up my purchases. He hands her the credit card and I'm too nervous about how much I spent to listen. I wonder where we will go next, while I wait.

"Come help me carry your bags," Jack orders.

I step forward and grab half of the bags and we leave the store. Jack sends a text and we head for the carpark to meet the limo. It's waiting on the side of the street as we approach. The driver takes the bags and places them in the trunk as we take our seats.

"Where are we going next?" I ask excitedly, getting caught up in the day.

"We're going to the spa to get your hair and skin taken care of. You'll need to follow any regimens they give you.

Afterwards, we'll go take care of your makeup needs." He watches me closely as he speaks.

"I don't wear makeup." I shake my head.

"You do now. Don't worry, they'll teach you how to apply it." He laughs, apparently finding joy in my misery.

"He's trying to help you fit in. That's a good thing," Kylah says, yawning.

"I feel like I'm losing myself." I stare out the window.

"I know it's all overwhelming, but it could be a positive experience if you let it." He frowns.

"I have my part to play. I guess I may as well play it well," I sigh, feeling overwhelmed but not wanting to admit it.

I wish my mom hadn't told me to be brave and not show weakness. It means I have to 'suck it up buttercup', as she used to say. We pull in front of a fancy day spa while I was lost in my own thoughts. Here we go, I think to myself.

CHAPTER FOUR

The driver opens the door and I climb out behind Jack. He gives me an encouraging smile then walks to the doors, so I follow like a lost puppy. I hate being so far outside of my comfort zone. He goes straight to the receptionist's desk, but I take the time to survey the area.

The monochromatic color scheme is both soft and severe. Shades of grey intermingle with the stark white walls and black pillars to the black-and-white marble floors. The duality of the place isn't lost on me. It's both inviting and cold.

"Appointment for Amelia Huntsman," Jack tells the receptionist.

"Ah, yes. Right this way," she says extending her arm.

I glance at Jack, who nods encouragingly, before following her. I straighten my spine and remember, show no weakness. The further into the spa we go, the warmer and richer the colors become. Leaving behind the cool tones and entering the warmth of the soothing tans, browns, and light greens.

"I know the lobby is a bit much." The receptionist chuckles.

"It is a bit intimidating." I nod my agreement.

"You'll start with hair then move on to skincare. Have fun," She gives me a warm smile and leaves me in front of a stylist.

"My name is Cassie; can I call you Amelia?" she asks, her face lights up as she smiles.

I nod, checking her over. She's tall with bright, fire engine red hair, shaved close to the head on one side and long on the other. Her blue eyes sparkle with mischief, and her high cheekbones are striking.

"Wow, we need to get your hair healthy!" she exclaims as she examines my hair. "What kind of hairstyle are you thinking?"

"I just want to keep it long." I dread all these new changes. This is something I can keep the same.

"We'll focus on the health of your hair and what products you need to use." She grins then teases me. "I was hoping you'd let me shave one side of your head."

I mull over her suggestion, even if it was in jest. My hair would still be long... and it would be a bold statement to match my new wardrobe...

"Actually, that sounds like a great idea! Will I be able to hide it?" I ask, feeling a sudden urge to be spontaneous.

"Yes, see how my hair is parted at the side? I move the part to the middle, and voila, shaved part hidden." She demonstrates, hiding her own side shave from view.

"Oh, I so need this now!" I exclaim, wanting something to make me feel edgier.

If I have to change everything about myself, I might as well be a little daring in this new life. Cassie parts my hair at the side and grabs her clippers.

"Are you sure? Once I start, there's no going back." She

raises an eyebrow, giving me a profoundly serious expression.

"Yes, just do it," I squeak, afraid that I'll back out if she gives me the chance.

I squeeze my eyes closed as she runs the clippers through my hair, shaving the side down. My heart pounds, and I wonder what I've just done until my mom's words come back to me. Be brave and show no weakness. *This is brave,* I tell myself.

"This better not shave my fur," Kylah huffs.

"I need to trim up the ends, but I won't take any length off," she explains as she works on my hair.

I open my eyes to glimpse the new cut, but she's already parted my hair back in the middle. I can't wait to see if I appear different. She trims the ends up the spins the chair around, scrutinizing me with an appraising eye.

"Now scoot and go get your hair washed to get rid of all the little hairs from the clipper," she orders, smacking my shoulder playfully with her comb.

I walk over to the sinks, where a girl waves me over to sit down.

These changes today are overwhelming, but I can use this new identity will be like an armor. I was a sporty girl before, always in jeans and t-shirts. Now I have a wardrobe that costs more than I can fathom, and I have to do hair and makeup. I'm just thankful some of those upgraded outfits are in my comfort zone.

She washes my hair, which feels like heaven. It always feels so good when someone else washes your hair. When she's done, I give her a smile and go back to Cassie's chair.

"Now, we will talk about styling and products," she says seriously.

She goes through the products I need to use to take better care of my hair and to style it.

"Now, it's time to see your new hair." Cassie smiles as she spins me around to face the mirror.

I look like me but different, my jaw drops. The shaved side gives me an edgy flair, nothing like I would have expected to see on me, but somehow, it's fitting. I ask how to style it like this, and she teaches me. She also shows me how to style my hair in a few different ways. I decide right then, if it's allowed, I only want Cassie doing my hair from now on.

"Ok, time to go get pampered." She chuckles.

"Pampered equals pain doesn't it?" I groan, not liking how evil said chuckle sounds.

"Have fun." She smiles and waves her fingers at me.

"Humans are all so strange," Kylah says, flicking her tail.

The shampoo girl leads me through the spa to another woman who hands me a robe and fuzzy sandals then leads me to a room.

"Please put these on and come back out," she states curtly, her face frozen in a sour expression.

"Wake me up when you're done with all these humans," Kylah sighs.

I sigh, another not so nice person. I hope she's not who I have to deal with the rest of the time. I finish undressing and step out, but the woman is nowhere in sight. A young woman comes running up.

"Amelia, right?" she asks, out of breath.

"That's me." I wave my fingers.

"Sorry, I got caught up with my last client. But, I'm here now. My name's Meagan. Can you follow me, please?" she asks, finally catching her breath.

I follow her through the spa area to a private room. She turns on the light, and I sit in the chair, scared of what will happen.

"We're just going to do a facial and basic skin care

routine. You're too young to need the works." She winks at me.

"Ok, I can handle that," I reply, inwardly letting out a sigh of relief.

I sit still as she plasters stuff on my face and takes it off to put more stuff on. It feels gross and relaxing at the same time. When she finishes, she hands me a bag full of products and explains how each one of them works. My head is spinning when she directs me back to the room my clothes are in.

Once I'm dressed, the curt woman leads me back to the front lobby where Jack is waiting. His eyes about bug out of his head when he sees me, then I remember my side shave is showing.

"I can cover it," I explain, suddenly feeling self-conscious.

"No, it's perfect. It'll let the other students know you have attitude and they can't mess with you. It's brilliant really, just shocked that's what you went for." He grins.

"You will act the part of a princess brilliantly," Jace whispers from the edge of my mind, causing Kylah to purr.

"Please say we are done and can go eat again?" I ask, my stomach growling again painfully.

"We can. We'll stay in town tonight and finish up tomorrow," he answers, giving me a sympathetic look.

We get in the limo and the driver takes us to the hotel. Jack checks us in, and the bellhop brings up all my purchases behind us.

"The driver was out picking up personal items and luggage while you were at the spa. I figured we could order room service since you will eat more than most would expect of a teenage girl," Jack explains fidgeting his hands again.

"Thank you," I reply, just wanting to get to the food.

"You need to feed us more often. Our metabolism is faster now," Kylah pouts, feeling our shared hunger.

We take the elevator to one of the top floors, and when the bellhop opens the door, it's a living room area with four doors leading off.

"We'll each take a bedroom, and you'll have a private bath," Jack explains after he tips the bellhop. "You can pick your room first."

I run over and open the first door; it's a king-size canopy bed with sheer white fabric hanging from it. The bedspread is also white. I move on to the next room, and it's a queen bed with a blue comforter. I run across the room and open the next door. It's a king bed with dark red bedspread and room accents. I choose this room. In the bathroom is a walk-in shower and a large soaking tub. I grin, thinking about soaking in the tub.

I run back out to the joint living space. There is a tiny kitchen off to one side, a table to eat at, and a large grey sectional couch facing a mounted flat screen TV over a gas fireplace.

"Did you choose that room?" Jack asks with a grin.

"Yeah," I reply smiling.

"Take your stuff in there and get it organized. You can pack your clothes, so we'll be ready to go tomorrow. I ordered food to be brought up. It should be here by the time you're done," he orders, unsure of himself.

"Fine, take all the fun out of shopping," I tease, preferring to be organized myself.

I lug all my purchases back to my room for the night and start unpacking them onto the bed. I finally get to inspect everything I got today. The outfits are all edgy but comfortable, just like my new haircut. Jeans with holes strategically ripped in them, bright red plaid pants, thin plaid long sleeve shirts, are just a few of the items. My favorite is a black t-shirt with red writing.

The saleswoman did a good job picking underwear sets to go with each outfit. I fold everything up and place them in piles to pack away. Jack knocks on the open door then brings in a three-piece, bright red luggage set and another luggage cart of stuff.

"I don't think everything will fit in here." I grimace but loving the luggage set.

"We'll make it work. Worst case, we'll need to get you more luggage. You'll need to pick a few handbags tomorrow. Girls will expect you to have more than one," he explains, shaking his head.

There's a knock at the door, so Jack leaves me to answer it. I grab the large bag and can fit all my clothes in it. It fits more than I expected. I can fit all my toiletries in the smallest bag, with room for makeup, so that leaves the middle bag for what's left on the luggage cart.

"Food's here," Jack calls out.

"Coming," I respond, excited to eat.

I leave the rest of the packing until I eat. The smells coming from the living room have my mouth watering. When I get to the table, he had ordered steaks, baked pota-toes, several vegetable sides, hamburgers, and fries.

"Dig in," he chuckles, his smile reaching his eyes.

He doesn't have to tell me twice. I grab a plate, load it up, and eat until my stomach is full. I feel better but tired.

"I'm going to finish packing and go to sleep," I yawn; suddenly, the exhaustion and weight of the day hits me.

"I think that's a good idea. You've been through a lot," he agrees, pity flashing across his eyes.

I feel like I'm falling into this change too comfortably. I know part of it is Kylah and her readiness to accept being with her clan, but it should be harder for me. I go back to my room and go through the bags on the cart. There's a high-end laptop, a tablet, and a cellphone in one bag, the other is full of bath products and deodorants. The last bag has basic school supplies in it. I pack all of it with the laptop and tablet in the middle-sized suitcase. Thankfully, it fits without unboxing them. I set the cellphone box on the bed and check the last bag on the cart. It's full of cases for the tablet and phone. My jaw drops at how much these cases cost.

Once I finish picking my jaw up off the ground, I pick out fresh undergarments and a nightgown and take advantage of the soaker tub. There's a jasmine and sweet pea bath oil, so I pour it in then climb into the nice, steamy water. I can feel my muscles relaxing. When the water cools, I drag myself out and get dressed. I find a toothbrush and toothpaste then remember my new skincare regimen. I sigh and grab those products. By the time I'm done, I lie down to a dreamless sleep.

I WAKE up to the smell of eggs and bacon. I jump up and run into the living area, my stomach growling again. Food is the only thing that I can think of.

"Why am I so hungry?" My stomach pangs making me wince.

"You're sixteen and your metabolism is that of a shifter now. Get used to it." Jack chuckles moving away from the food to give me access.

I grab a plate and finish it just as quickly. With a full belly, I make my way back into my room and decide on a shower. Today is a big day for me. It's the day I see my new home. I feel the nerves building inside of me as the warm water runs over my body. It partially helps to relax the anxiety but doesn't ease it. After completing my new skin care routine, I pick out an outfit for the day. I put my dirty clothes in with my electronics and debate on taking my old clothes with me. I decide finally to leave them behind. It wouldn't go well if someone were to find them. I grab one of the phone cases and put it on before powering up the new phone. It's already set up and programmed with Jack's number in it. I put it in my pocket and make sure I have everything packed back up then wheel my luggage out to the living room.

"That was fast!" Jack exclaims with a smile.

"I tried," I mutter, not looking forward to more makeover stuff.

"All you have left is to get makeup and fitted for your school uniforms," Jack replies sympathetically.

"Let's go then," I yawn, not wanting to do anymore and feeling the urge to run.

"That's contagious." He yawns back and gives me a wink.

"I wish I could go run. I have all this energy that is just coiled right in my center," I sigh as I follow him to the door.

"When we get home, remind me and we will," he replies, surprising me.

He places both of our luggage sets on the cart and we leave the suite. On the elevator down, I begin to panic. Everything's happening so fast, and I just want to go home.

"Slow down your breathing, you can do this. You're stronger than this, and you'll do fine," Jack coaches.

I rein in my panic and calm down. "Thank you."

"It's a lot to take in. You're doing really well," he replies earnestly; his lips pulled up in a sympathetic smile.

We meet the driver in the lobby, and he has the limo pulled up already. He takes the luggage cart and loads everything up while we get in.

"First to get makeup, then we'll get you fitted for uniforms. Afterwards, we'll grab lunch and then fly back to the island. I was teasing about the boat before." He chuckles, glancing out of the corner of his eyes to gauge my reaction. I roll my eyes but smile.

I've never been a girl to wear makeup, but I'm determined to get this right. Even if I have to practice at it. I sigh and gaze out the window. It's so strange seeing so many people in the same place. We finally stop in front of a large store that only sells makeup. I take a deep breath and follow Jack in. He stops at a counter towards the middle of the store.

"She'll need everything to get her made up and directions on how to apply it," he tells the girl behind the counter.

"This is so silly," Kylah yawns then turns around and lays back down.

"I totally agree, but Jack says I need it to fit in," I explain to her.

"Come sit here." She grins, patting the chair.

I spend the next thirty minutes with her putting things on my face and explaining how they work. When she finishes, she lets me examine myself in the mirror and my jaw drops. I look amazing. She played off my hair and clothes and gave me darker makeup. I love it.

"Thank you," I grin at her.

"You're welcome," she replies then goes to ring up my purchases.

Jack pays for them, and we get back in the limo. I drift off to sleep on the way to the next store, but jolt awake when he touches my arm.

"All we have to do here is get you measured, then we can go back to the plane or eat first, your choice," he smiles.

"Let's go to the plane. We can eat when we get there?" I ask, not starving yet.

"Sounds like a solid plan," he replies, a grateful expression gliding across his face.

I follow him out of the limo into a small, unmarked building. Inside is a boring white-walled room with brown industrial carpet. An older woman comes out of the curtained door. I can smell she's a shifter, that's new.

"She's a panther like us," Kylah purrs happily.

"Is this Amelia?" she asks; her eyes crinkled in a smile.

"That's me," I reply smiling, Kylah's happiness rubbing off on me.

"Come with me, and we'll get you measured," she orders, her eyes crinkle in a smile.

I follow her into the back room where she has me stand on a small raised platform in the middle of the room. She measures every part of me before dismissing me. I walk back out from where Jack is waiting, and we get in the limo and go to the airport.

CHAPTER FIVE

The driver takes care of our luggage as we board the plane. My stomach is in knots. Somehow, flying to the island is making this all more real. It was easy to pretend the shopping trip was a vacation... that I would be returning home when it was over.

A single tear slips down my cheek. I wipe it away and straighten my back. I will show no weakness, I remind myself. I need to quit being a whiny crybaby and face the music. Things will never go back to what they used to be. This IS my life now and the sooner I accept that, the easier it will be.

I fasten my seat belt and wait for takeoff. It doesn't take long, and we're in the air.

"I don't enjoy flying at all," Kylah huffs, pacing anxiously in the back of my head.

"Me either, but you get used to it the more you do it," Jace says, trying to calm her.

Flying over the ocean is beautiful; though, it doesn't take long and we're preparing to land on the island. It's only a fifteen-minute flight. There are sandy beaches surrounding the east side of the island with lots of green further in. My panther purrs at the sight. I press my face to the window as we land, trying to see everything at once. There's a large stone building hidden in the trees. A sense of foreboding settles in my stomach when my eyes land on it.

"That's the school." Jack points to the stone building.

"It's creepy," I reply, a shiver runs down my spine.

"It's nicer on the inside." He shrugs, seeming indifferent.

"Did you go there?" I ask curious, trying to picture him there.

"Yes, all Huntsman are required to go." He nods.

"I guess it'll be ok then," I sigh, not looking forward to starting over with a bunch of new teenagers.

"You'll have a few days before you start. We'll study some clan history, so you won't be too far behind. Students don't start at the academy until they are sixteen. So, you'll be joining the incoming class," he explains, patting my shoulder.

"That makes me feel better, even though everyone already knows everyone else," I reply sadly, feeling sorry for myself.

"Remember, there are cities set up around the world that we live in so we can police the shifters better. Those enforcers have kids that are sent here when it's time as well." Jack smiles, easing my nerves.

"Hopefully, I can blend in. I'm just going to hold my head up and act like my new style." I grin, trying to fake confidence.

"There's the spirit." Jack winks.

It works... that's good to know. I'll just pretend I belong until I do.

When we land, there's a black car waiting for us. Jack's eyes widen, but quickly shows no emotion. I wonder what he saw to startle him as we exit the plane. His face quickly shifts from the teasing, light-hearted man to one of serious stature.

Was it all a ruse to loll me into a sense of comfort to get me here with less of a fight?

We approach a tall thin, man with long, wavy black hair, standing next to the car. His eyes are black orbs, and his face is wearing a scowl that exaggerates its severe angles.

"Hello Sir, I didn't expect to see you until tomorrow," Jack says, standing stiffly.

"He isn't nice," Kylah growls. *"Neither is his lion."*

"I wanted to meet our newest member in person." The man smiles, but it doesn't reach his eyes.

"My name is Heathcliff, and I'll be your headmaster. You will call me Sir. Do you understand?" he demands, no room for argument.

"Yes, Sir," I deadpan, meeting his eyes and forgetting that I shouldn't.

"Good. I understand you'll be staying with Jack until school starts. Make sure he acquaints you with the rules." He sneers down his nose.

He walks away, getting into a car close to the airplane. Jack gives a visible sigh of relief. Once Heathcliff is out of sight, Jack pivots and stares at me.

"Stay off his radar. He's brutal." Jack shudders, his eyes glaze over in remembrance.

"Bad memories?" I ask, teasing him.

"You don't even want to know. It's not been that long since I graduated." He grins, bumping my shoulder with his.

"How old are you?" I stop and examine him.

"How old do you think I am?" he retorts, in fake shock.

"Um. Maybe twenty-five?" I answer trying to guess based on how he's acted so far.

"You wound me. I just turned twenty-one a few days ago." He grabs his chest dramatically.

"Wow, I thought you were more than five years older than

me. Why did you agree to take responsibility for me when you should be out living it up?" I ask, perplexed.

"Everyone needs someone…" His eyes cloud over momentarily as if lost in a memory. "Besides, you'll be at school most of the time." He grins, but it doesn't reach his eyes.

"Don't remind me," I pout, not wanting to think about that.

"Let's go home." He changes the subject for me.

We climb into the backseat of the waiting car, and I lean my head against the window. Jack is talking, but I don't really hear what he's saying. I watch the town as we drive through, and you can tell no humans live here. There are shifters walking around in animal form among the people. The shops all have entrances for both animal and human forms. It's unlike anything I've ever seen before.

"This is the best home," Kylah says in awe, watching along through my eyes.

"Amelia?" Jack says my name, trying to get my attention.

"Huh, oh sorry. I was watching the town," I mumble, embarrassed to have tuned him out.

"I asked what you would like to eat for lunch. We can eat out or order food at the house," he patiently explains again.

"I'd rather eat at the house," I whisper, feeling self-conscious now that we're here.

"It's a lot to adjust to, but you'll get there." He pats me on the back, trying to be helpful.

"I will, and after today, I'll be strong and brave. Today though, I can't be," I sigh, trying to figure out how I will do this, when I can't even figure out who I am.

"We are strong and a panther. No need to be weak," Kylah huffs, not understanding my conflicting feelings.

"You'll find your place here. Just don't let anyone get you down," Jack replies, sympathy clear on his face.

We pull up in front of a bright green bungalow, the yard immaculately kept. I try not to laugh but fail miserably. The first impression is his house was slimed. The shutters and front door are even this almost fluorescent green color.

"Don't laugh; it wasn't my choice," he sulks, with his arms across his chest. His lip even sticks out a bit.

"My dad always said if you leave your lip out like that a bird will poop on it." I giggle, and it progresses into a full-on belly laugh.

"Come on, let's get inside." He gives a small smile.

"Why is your house this horrible shade of green?" I ask, trying not to giggle anymore.

"It involves alcohol and bad bets." He grins. "Never make a bet you're not willing to see through."

We grab our bags from the trunk of the car and go inside. It's clear that this is a bachelor pad from the moment my eyes adjust. The walls are bare and painted an off white. There's a dark brown couch and a coffee table in the living room, with a big screen TV across from them.

"Let me take you on a tour," he says, extending his arm in front of him.

"Ok," I smirk, trying not to laugh.

He leads us into the kitchen, which is cleaner than it should be. It's as if it's only there for display, with its fresh white cabinets and immaculate stovetop.

"Do you even know how to cook?" I raise an eyebrow.

"Do you have a filter?" he responds, grinning.

"I've filtered a lot of my thoughts, thank you." I put my hands on my hips. I can't believe he thinks I don't have a filter.

"This way to the bedrooms," he says, waiting for me to follow him.

"Where do you eat?" I ask, not seeing a table anywhere.

"On the couch." He shakes his head. "Isn't it obvious?"

I roll my eyes and follow him to the hallway off the kitchen.

"The door to the right is my room. I have a private bathroom, so this middle door will be your bathroom." He opens said door.

It's a simple all white bathroom, with a clear shower curtain. I shrug and close the door then move on to the room on the left.

"This is your bedroom now. We can get furniture and bedding that suits you. Feel free to decorate it however you like. When you're not at school, this is where you'll live." He puts his hands in his pockets and rocks back onto his heels.

"Home," Kylah purrs.

"No, we left home to come here," I think to her then smile at Jack. "Thank you," I reply, surprised that I mean it.

"I'll just go order food. Pizza, or does Chinese sound better?"

"Pizza, extra meat, please."

"Go ahead and get settled in then come out to the living room whenever you're ready."

I drag my luggage into the bedroom as he walks off to order food. I shut the door behind me and collapse on the twin bed pushed up against the far wall. It's the only thing in the room, with a white comforter on it. Very boring is how I would describe the room.

I lie on the bed staring at the popcorn ceiling trying to make faces out of the different-sized dots. It's a good distraction from thinking about my current life. Everything is happening so fast I can't process, but maybe that's a good thing. I tire of my little game and begin unpacking.

One thing my mom taught me was to be tidy. I can't stand a mess in my personal space. I wish I had drawers to put some of my clothes, but it's not a big deal to leave them in the bag for now. I'll ask Jack for them when I go to the living room. I add vanity to the list; I need somewhere to put on all this makeup.

I lay out the electronics on the bed but decide there's no point fiddling with them when I don't have the Wi-Fi password yet. I place the luggage in the closet then go to the living room to see how long the food will be.

"Are you getting settled in all right?" Jack asks as I enter the living room.

"Um, I had enough hangers, but I don't have any drawers or anywhere to do my makeup," I reply awkwardly, not wanting to ask for more things.

"We'll go shopping tomorrow for your bedroom furniture. You have a week before school starts so we have plenty of time to get everything you need to be settled. More clothes if you need them," he explains, smiling so big his eyes wrinkle.

"Thank you. How long until the pizza?" I ask, just as there's a knock at the door.

"That should be it," he chuckles. I can tell he's a naturally happy person, and under different circumstances, I think I would like him. Right now, all I feel is resentment that I'm trying hard to hide.

"You need to feed us better," Kylah flicks her tail in annoyance.

He returns with two large pizzas and sets them on the coffee table before heading into the kitchen and returning with plates. I open the first box and it smells delicious and is full of meat toppings. I grab a piece and take a bite. Bad idea, I feel the skin behind my front teeth on the roof of my mouth burn.

"Cold water," I hiss, through the pain.

"Maybe I should be the one feeding us," Kylah snickers.

"Be nice," I chide.

Jack laughs. "Burn your mouth?"

"Not funny jerk," I growl. I'm in pain, and he's making jokes.

"Here," he says, handing me a glass of ice water.

"Thank you," I reply before taking a big drink and holding it in my mouth.

Ah instant relief. Now that my mouth is better, I blow on the pizza then take another bite. I'm starving again. I make short work of devouring the entire large pizza.

"Wow! I've never eaten that much at once before!" I exclaim, feeling like a pig.

"Get used to it, your metabolism is running at a much faster speed." Jack laughs, acting as if I should know this already.

"Why didn't the bear shifters have this issue?" I ask, not remembering anyone eating more than normal.

"Because bears aren't their own being. They are a half concept," Kylah replies.

"They aren't the same, I guess. Not sure. All cat shifters eat a lot more," he shrugs.

"That's interesting. I'll have to ask my mom. That reminds me, do you have Wi-Fi? I need to set up the computer you bought." I search for an excuse to be alone.

"Let me get the password for you." He stands up and exits the room.

He returns quickly with a neon yellow sticky, a serious of numbers and letters scribbled across it. I grab it and thank him as I rush to my room. It doesn't take long to get the computer and tablet set up, leaving me with some time to call my mom. I miss them so much it hurts. I'm still upset they lied to me, but they are my family and I hate that they took me away.

"Hello?" My mom's voice comes through the line.

"Hi Mom, this is my new number," I say, my chest aching when her voice washes over me.

"Amelia, it's so good to hear your voice," she gushes.

Be strong, Lia you can do this! I repeat in my head.

"I miss you," I force my emotions down, swallowing them like a lump in my throat.

"We miss you too, sweetheart." Mom's voice warbles.

"How are Dad and Josh doing?" I chew on the inside of my cheek. Why does this feel so strange?

"They are as well as can be expected. We are all just learning what our new reality is." Her voice warbles. "How are you settling in there?"

"I'm trying to be strong." I sigh, then ask what I've been wondering. "Do bear shifters eat more once they turn sixteen?"

"No, but I've heard some types of shifters do. I take it you're eating a lot." She giggles. It makes my heart hurt to hear but also reassuring that she can.

"I ate an entire large pizza, and I could eat more," I admit, almost giggling myself. "I start school in a week, and I'm scared I can't do this."

"Amelia, I did not raise a coward. You will be fine. Just hold your head high and pretend you're just at boarding school." she chastises me.

"I'll try; this is all just so confusing," I reply, my face aching from trying to keep my emotions in check.

"You'll do great. You're a smart girl, so you'll figure out how to navigate the world you're in now," she says matter-of-factly, her tone leaving no room to argue. "And always remember, we love you no matter what."

"Thank you, I needed to hear that. I love you," I say, missing home.

"I love you too, sweetie," she replies, her voice sad.

"Ok, well I'll call you soon," I say uncomfortably, not knowing what to talk about.

"Don't forget we're always here for you," she replies then hangs up.

"See, your old family knows this is where we should be. Try to be happy like me," Kylah attempts to comfort me.

"That's easier said than done," I sigh, not engaging her any further.

I get the computer out and start trying to find information on the Huntsman clan. I should have known it would be a futile search. We as shifters try to keep ourselves hidden. I know I'll have to talk to Jack about the information I need, but I'm just not ready to fake being nice again. I lay down and stare up at the ceiling, but curiosity gets the best of me. I groan inwardly at myself and get up, returning to the living room.

"Let's go pick out your furniture," Jack suggests when he sees me.

"Ok, that sounds like a good idea, but you said we would do it tomorrow?" I can't wait to have somewhere to put my stuff.

"You look like you need a distraction." He grabs his car keys.

I follow him out through the kitchen to the back door to the carport. I stop short and stare at the little silver Prius. I was expecting something different. I look back and forth between Jack and the car, trying to reconcile the two in my mind.

"Hey, we should all think about the environment," he says, raising his eyebrow, waiting for me to contradict him.

"Why can't we run? I saw other cats!" Kylah roars, wanting out.

"You're not ready to be in control of her, and she's not ready for you to be in control," Jace answers.

"I said nothing," I reply, lifting my hands up in a shrug.

"You were thinking it," he mutters under his breath.

"I think you need to explain this knowing my thoughts thing already, because they aren't the same as Kylah's," I confront him, getting irritated.

"When we get back to the house, I'll explain," he sighs, acting like he doesn't want to explain at all.

"You better," I mumble then let it go for the time being.

We drive downtown to Main Street. My first thought is how cliché. There's a furniture store mid-block that we park in front of. Like the rest of the town, it has two doors, one for animal form and one for human form. It will take some getting used to.

Inside, the store is huge. Everything in the store appears to be made from actual wood: cherry, oak, cedar; no cheap pressed board found here. I wander through the furniture, not caring if Jack follows me or not. The living room furniture is at the front of the store, followed by dining sets. The bedroom furniture is all the way in the back.

"Hey, you should get a dining table while we're here," I tease Jack, doubting he would want one.

"Ok, pick one out," he replies grinning.

I see a bar height table in a dark walnut with high-back chairs. "This one."

"Wow! You picked one that a guy would use!" he exclaims incredulously.

"Well yeah. You are a bachelor," I snark at him. He should know I wouldn't pick out something girly for his place.

I grin at him, to show I'm kind of kidding then make my way back to the bedroom section. There are several styles to choose from, it's overwhelming. I walk around and check out each piece and try to imagine myself using them. I come to the end of the first row, and I'm in love at first sight. It's an off-white color with headboard, dresser, and vanity. The vanity has five drawers to store things and a big mirror with two moveable side mirrors. I'm in love.

"This set," I say confidently.

"Let me find the owner and have it all delivered," Jack replies, and takes off.

I sit at the vanity and imagine myself putting on makeup there. It's perfect, but too bad I can't take it to school with me. Jack returns shortly with another man.

"I forgot to ask; do you want a matching set at school?" Jack inquires, grinning stupidly.

"Can I really?" I ask, becoming giddy at the thought.

"Yes, we need to get your furniture ordered anyway," the store owner replies. "I'll have everything delivered today."

"Oh wow! That's fast!" I exclaim.

"Let's get going. I figured we should go grocery shopping, so you have food to eat this week. I imagine you'll be snacking a lot," Jack teases.

"You just want to avoid going home," I accuse him. I'm sure he's avoiding answering my question.

"Guilty, but you still need food, so two birds with one stone," he grins again. I roll my eyes.

"Give him time, he doesn't open up easily," Jace explains.

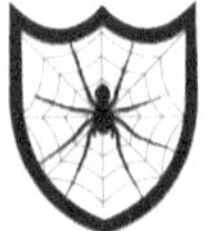

CHAPTER SIX

The meat department in this grocery store is the largest I've ever seen. I follow Jack through the aisles while he loads the cart with more food than I've ever seen my mother buy for our family.

"I will only be here for a week, right?" I ask, surprised at how much food he's buying.

"Yeah, this should get us through to when you leave. If not, we'll come back for more," he replies, taking inventory of the cart.

"You think we'll eat that much?" I ask. I can't imagine eating that much food, although I have been starving lately.

"I know we'll eat at least this much," he grins. I swear that man can hear my thoughts.

My stomach growls, making him chuckle. "Let's check out and get you home to feed you."

"I offered to hunt for us," Kylah says in an irritated tone.

When he says home, I withdraw, not allowing myself to think of his house as home. Home is back with my parents. I follow him out to the car after he finishes paying, trying to push my feelings down but failing miserably.

"It is home. Get used to it, please," Kylah growls softly.

"Look, I'm used to my house being home. I don't mean for you to call it that immediately, but hopefully, someday, it'll be your home away from home," he explains, noticing my broodiness.

"I don't want anywhere else to be my home. I'm trying to be brave and strong like my mom told me to be, but it's hard," I sob uncontrollably. I've been bottling everything up, and it forces its way out and I can't stop it now that it's started.

Jack drives us home in silence, well him silent and me crying and sniffling. When we pull up to the carport, he runs inside, but I'm not ready to move. I just sit in the car and feel sorry for myself. Why should I be strong? I'm just a teenager. I shouldn't have to deal with this crap. I get angry.

I open the car door and crawl out. I can feel Kylah lurking just under my skin, and she wants free. She's not waiting any longer. I strip my clothes off, not wanting to get stuck in these tight jeans. She bursts free as soon as I get the second leg free.

Jack comes out of the house and shifts as soon as he sees me. His leopard markings are evenly spaced, with a tiny tuft of white fur on his chest.

We take off running down the easement behind the house then glance over our shoulder to see if he is following. He overtakes us in three strides.

"This way." Jace swings his head in the direction we should run.

It feels so good to stretch our legs and run off some tension from the past few days. Kylah finally wears out and climbs a tree to nap. Jack follows us up and nips at our leg. He doesn't want us napping in the tree, apparently. She growls at him but follows him down and we walk back to the house. He shifts back when we hit the yard.

"Kylah you have to let Lia back in control," Jace says.

"Make me," she growls.

"You don't have control over your panther at all, do you?" Jack narrows his eyes.

I try to picture my human form, and Kylah turns her growl towards me. I put my foot down and try harder to shift. Finally, she relents. She will learn if she can be stubborn so can I. As she backs down, I'm able to shift.

"Apparently not," I sigh. Numbness is taking over, which I can't decide is welcome or not.

"I shouldn't have to listen to someone as weak and emotional as you," she huffs then lays down, her tail flicking in annoyance.

"What made you shift?" he sits down next to me.

"I was angry. I don't understand why I have to deal with all of this, and I just want to go home and pretend like none of this ever happened," I explain, feeling defeated.

"I can understand that. I would have left you if I could have," he replies, his voice betraying the regret he feels.

"Why didn't you then?" I ask, accusingly.

"We belong here," Kylah says.

"Because you don't have a speck of white on you. If anyone reported you after I left you there, they would have killed me for lying and brought you here anyway," he growls, his face turning a shade of crimson and the vein on his forehead popping out.

"Why are you mad? You weren't the one who thought they were a bear then ripped away from the only life they knew!" I scream at him, my head pounding. I can feel my pulse in my temples.

"Calm down, let's get the groceries inside, and I'll explain everything." His shoulders slump in defeat.

I calm down as guilt gnaws at my stomach. Something is eating at him. Something I'm positive he doesn't want to talk about. Now, I'm more than curious. I quickly unload the car and help Jack put the groceries away. When we finish, he leads me to the couch. We settle in and he sits quietly for a moment as if he's gathering his thoughts. He opens his mouth to speak, but the doorbell rings. I groan audibly.

"I'll still explain; that's probably the furniture," he says as he goes to answer the door.

I cross my arms across my chest and throw myself back into the couch. The furniture owner and a teenage guy come in carrying the table I picked out earlier. He's cute with shaggy light brown hair and hazel eyes. The strong jaw is softened by dimples when his full lips tip up into a smile.

"Tiger," Kylah opens her mouth, scenting him.

"Sorry, did you say something," I stumble on my words, realizing he's staring at me smiling.

"I said nice to meet you; my name's Vance," he replies, grinning ear to ear.

"Amelia, but everyone used to call me Lia," I reply, feeling stupid. I can't seem to get it together around him.

"I'll call you Lia then," he winks. "I'll be starting my first year at Nightfall this year too. It's a bit nerve-wracking. I hope Dad can survive without me." He grins and points over his shoulder at the older man.

"You're nervous too?" I ask, shocked that anyone who lived here would be.

"Yeah, they don't tell us much about what happens up there to keep everyone on an even playing field. I hope it's not too crazy," he explains, rubbing the back of his neck.

"Vance, this furniture will not move itself," his dad says from the hallway.

"Sorry, I got to..." he replies and points to the hallway and walks off.

"I like his tiger," Kylah replies.

"I have a name; it's Montoya." Vance's tiger introduces himself.

"Nice to meet you Montoya," I reply, but don't get a response.

I sit on the couch while they carry out the old bed from my room then all the new furniture. I can't pinpoint these conflicting emotions. Part of me is excited to have these new things, but the other part of me feels guilty for being excited. I would gladly give everything up to go home, but is it wrong for me to enjoy what I have since I'm stuck here? What a moral quandary I've found myself in. I should call my mom later and ask her opinion.

While I'm lost in my own thoughts, the rest of the furniture is brought in and set up. Vance walks back in the room with his hands in his pockets; his grey t-shirt fits tight and stops where his worn jeans start.

"So, I can give you my number if you want to do something before school starts," Vance offers, rocking back and forth on his heels with his thumbs in his front belt loops.

"Oh, yeah. That would be great," I reply, giving the first genuine smile I think I've mustered.

I hand him my cell phone and relief passes over his face. He hands me his phone, and we trade contacts.

"My dad's waiting on me, but I'll text you," he grins as he walks out the door.

"We like them; that's good," Kylah purrs.

I get up and rush into my new room to see how everything turned out. It's even better than I remembered. But there are no pillows or bedding to be seen. Crap, I don't even remember shopping for any.

"I'll answer your questions then we'll go get what you need," Jack says behind me, causing me to jump and Kylah to growl through my throat. "Easy there; let's go eat while I talk."

I follow him to the new dining table and wait while he

gathers us everything from beef jerky to fruit. I grab a stick of jerky as he sits down.

"Ok, so how much do you know about the Huntsman clan?" he asks, a wrinkling between his eyebrows showing how hard he's thinking.

"They're the rulers over all shifters, and if someone commits a crime, they take care of it. Oh, and they're all a member of one of the cat species," I answer, not recalling anything else.

"That's a good start. There are four royal houses: the panthers, the tigers, the lions, and the leopards. Any other type of shifter is automatically common class, but you'll find some of the cat shifters can be common class as well," he stops and gathers his thoughts. "Now there are royal, noble, and common classes. Royal class shifters are easy to tell in their shifted form. The panthers are solid black, the leopards have a distinct shape spot, the tigers have a distinct stripe pattern, and the lions have no white patches."

"Ok, this is good information to know," I say hesitantly, not wanting him to stop speaking.

"The common class of shifters are just that, common. They can shift and that's it, but some in the noble and royal classes have an extra ability. Mine is to read the thoughts of others. It's not like I hear directly what you think, more of a general feeling," he explains uncomfortably. "If you were to develop one, it wouldn't be for several years."

"Well, stay out of my head then!" I scream, feeling violated.

"It's not like that! I only hear thoughts that are being projected loudly, and girl, you've been thinking loud thoughts. Like how you want to bash my head in right now," he replies, trying to defuse the situation.

"He's not wrong; besides, I hear all your thoughts too," Kylah comments, confused as to why I'm upset.

"That's not exactly what I was thinking, but close enough," I mumble feeling better that he can't hear what I'm thinking.

"Ok, so to the part I really don't want to talk about," he sighs, gathering his thoughts, the creases in his forehead deepening. He slouches forward aging himself by years.

"I'm of the noble class as was my brother. When we finish school, we have the choice to take a limited number of positions based on how we scored in school. We both scored high on becoming enforcers. That's what I am now. So, we decided we would work at the same job. He got a call like the one I received for you. A shifter changed, and she turned into a cat instead of a wolf. Adoptions and hidden pregnancies happen," he stops, his eyes lost in a memory only he can see.

I wait patiently for him to talk again, not wanting to interrupt the moment he's having.

"Well, he arrived, and it was a solid black panther girl, much like you. He didn't want to disrupt her life, so he reported back that she was only common then left her be. A week later someone reported back to the queens that there was a black panther roaming around that area. They sent someone else to check it out and killed her and my brother." He finishes choking on his words. He hunches over and seems to be reliving the memory.

"Why did they kill them both?" I whisper, feeling awful for forcing him to talk now that I've heard it.

"They killed him because he didn't report her to them, and they killed her because she went feral before they found her. There's a reason the cats all go to Nightfall Academy." He stares me directly in my eye.

"So, if you wouldn't have brought me back, I would have likely gone feral and had to be killed?" I shriek.

"Your alpha was strong enough to probably contain you, but it could have happened, yes," he replies, regaining some of his former composure, though his eyes are still haunted.

"I'm sorry I've been so hard on you. I don't want us to die, and I'm sorry about your brother. He sounds like he was a good man," I whisper, placing my hand on his forearm in sympathy.

"Enough talk of the past. Let's just be happy we both have a future." He stands up and claps his hands together. From the set of his jaw, I know there will be no further discussion about this.

"Let's go get bedding?" I shrug my shoulders and offer a tiny smile.

"Come on then." He gives a hint of a grin and shakes his head.

We ride back downtown to a store that sells a bit of everything. I get out of the car, staying silent, lost in thought. Jack follows me and the silence is tense but not enough that I want to break it. As I examine the bedding sets, one catches my attention, and I know it's perfect. It's sea-foam green with silver filigree covering it. I grab it and the light grey, high thread count cotton sheets. I'm set.

"Don't forget to grab a set for school," Jack reminds me quietly.

"Oh yeah, thanks," I mumble. I totally forgot I'm setting up two new residences there for a minute.

We check out and ride silently back to the house. After hearing his story, I decided I need to be even more determined to stay strong and be brave. It's better than being dead, and like mom said, *Just pretend you're going to boarding school. Leave the rest out of it.*

"You'll do fine Lia; you're tougher than I would have been," Jack says, his eyes echoing the sincerity in his voice.

I head to my room immediately after we park and begin making my bed and setting up my room. I'm glad to unpack everything from the suitcases and put them in drawers and on the vanity. I begin to feel like I can do this. This can be my space, and I can fake this. My stomach betrays me and lets me know I haven't eaten for a few hours, so I reluctantly head to the kitchen.

My mom taught me how to cook so I want to make a meal for us. I search for his cookware and find nothing but one small frying pan and a spatula.

"Where's the rest of your cookware?" I yell, not seeing him in the living room.

"There's a frying pan," he yells back from his bedroom.

"You need more than that to cook with!" I exclaim frustrated that I can't make anything with just a frying pan.

"We can shift, and I can eat it raw," Kylah offers.

"Eww no," I reply, internally rolling my eyes at her.

"How about we get takeout tonight, then you can go buy cookware tomorrow?" he asks, grinning widely as he comes out of his bedroom.

"This was an excuse to eat takeout again wasn't it?" I accuse, narrowing my eyes at him and crossing my arms over my chest.

"You caught me, but I'm excited to have a home-cooked meal," he chuckles and grabs menus out of the cabinet next to the fridge then offers them to me. "Lady's choice."

"Um, Chinese," I reply after perusing the options. I'm easy to please. "Surprise me."

CHAPTER SEVEN

*H*e grabs his phone to order, and I head to my bedroom to call my mom. Now that I understand the worst case, I decide that I will make the best of this situation. Hearing her give me permission will set my mind at ease though.

"Amelia, how are you?" Mom answers with excitement in her voice.

"I'm doing good. I have everything I need to start school now and to set up where I have to stay on breaks. I've decided I will make the best of this and try to enjoy myself. Is that ok?" I ask, hoping with all my heart she agrees.

"Sweetie; we only want the best for you. Hopefully, you'll be able to come visit when school is out," she replies, her tone soothing.

"Thank you, Mommy. I really needed to hear that. I don't know how much I'll be able to call once I'm at school, but if I'm allowed to keep my phone, I'll at least text you updates," I say relieved that she agrees.

"I love you and I can't wait to hear about all of your adventures." A slight quiver betraying her happy tone.

"I love you too," I reply, my voice quivering because I'm trying not to cry.

We hang up, and I go back out to the living room to wait on food. I sit on the couch and download games on my phone. I'm in the middle of a game of *Candy Crush* when a text comes through.

Vance: Do you have plans tomorrow?

Me: I have to pick out cookware. Jack has none here.

Vance: I'm off tomorrow. We could go do something fun.

Me: That would be awesome. What time?

Vance: How about lunchtime? We can grab food then go.

Me: Great, I'll see you then.

"I'm going to go see the town with Vance tomorrow and have lunch," I tell Jack, hoping he doesn't tell me I can't.

"That would be good; maybe you can meet some other kids your age," he replies with a grin.

"It would be nice to know a few people before I start school with them," I say, agreeing that it would make starting easier.

I'm lost in level twelve of *Candy Crush* when the doorbell rings and Jack goes to answer the door. The smell of Chinese wafts through the air as the bags are passed across the threshold, and I hurry to the kitchen, retrieving plates and silverware to set up at the table. He sets the bags filled with containers on the table and it all smells so delicious. We waste no time opening up every container and piling the food onto our plates. A short time later, I'm scraping the last bit of fried rice off my plate.

"I can't believe I ate all of that!" I exclaim, still not accepting my new appetite.

"You're eating for both of us, quit acting so naïve," Kylah huffs turning her back to me.

"You've got to quit saying that, Lia. It will not change," he chuckles, poking fun at me. "Let's watch a movie."

"After I wash up," I reply, rolling my eyes.

"You don't have to do that. I'll get to it later," he says, a guilty expression crosses his face.

"I won't be able to enjoy the movie, and besides, it's better to just get it done with," I reply, sounding like my mother. I giggle at that thought. "Go pick the movie; it won't take me long."

I load the dishwasher and throw away the containers. When I make it to the living room, he has *Ready Player One* pulled up. I sit down and play on my phone through the movie. Not really my type of movie.

"I'm hungry," I say when the movie finishes.

"I'll go get some snacks," he chuckles, getting up and going to the kitchen.

I follow, wanting to help, but he waves me off. I sit at the table and wait while he loads it up with tons of food again; I munch on trail mix and veggies this time, until my stomach stops hurting.

"I'm going to bed; don't forget, we need to go buy cookware tomorrow," I say, covering a yawn.

"Goodnight. Do you want to go for a run in the morning?" he asks, scratching his neck.

"Sure, that sounds like a good plan. Wake me up when you're ready to go," I reply as I get up and walk back to my bedroom. I grab everything I need and take a quick shower then fall asleep as soon as my head hits the pillow.

"Wake up sleepy head, time for a run," Jack says from the doorway.

"Coming," I groan, then hold the pillow over my head.

I get up and put on some yoga pants and a t-shirt. I grab

my running shoes, the only thing left from my old life, and I'm ready to go.

We exit through the kitchen and take the same path we ran in animal form the previous day. It feels great to get out and stretch my legs. I hadn't realized how cramped up I was until I started running. I let go of thinking and just let my mind still while I stretch my muscles.

"Thank you, we needed to burn off energy," Kylah says, her ear flicking.

I'm famished by the time we get back to the house. I grab the one frying pan and start scrambling eggs while Jack makes the toast. I'm getting excited thinking about hanging out with Vance today. A friend before I go into a new school will make this so much easier.

"Do you know what you and Vance are planning on doing today?" Jack asks as we sit down to eat.

"Besides eat lunch, no. He didn't say," I reply between bites.

"Keep your cell phone on you and no shifting." He narrows his eyes.

"I'll try my hardest not to shift, but she's forced me to twice," I whisper, scared to leave the house now.

"Glad you finally recognize my superiority," Kylah says sitting up straight.

"You aren't superior; she just hasn't learned," Jace tells her sternly.

"It will be fine. Just don't shift intentionally, ok?" he asks, giving me a half smile.

"I won't," I reply through a yawn. I put my dish in the dishwasher and go back to bed for a while.

I wake up and realize I slept longer than I had intended. I only have thirty minutes to get ready before Vance shows up. I hop in the shower and rush through my new skin care routine. I realize I don't like all this extra work getting ready each day that this new life brings. I get my hair and makeup done in record time and not a minute too soon. Vance knocks on the door as I'm putting on the final touches.

"Lia, Vance is here," Jack yells from the front door.

"There's a strange female leopard with him," Kylah growls, not liking it.

"Hush and give her a chance," I snap at her.

"Coming," I answer, rolling my eyes since I already knew he was here.

I rush out to meet him and he has a short girl with him. I expect to see her from Kylah's warning, but I freeze for a minute not knowing how to react. I feel jealous, but he's not mine, so I have no right to be.

"Oh, hello," I say, trying to hide my initial shock. The girl is maybe five-one with a purple pixie cut. She dresses much in the same fashion as I am, with a slight punk theme, but she takes it one-step further with a piercing in her brow, slightly turned-up nose, and lip.

"Hi Lia. Can I call you Lia? I know we will be the best of friends. Vance told me you just moved here, and I said I just have to come along to meet my new best friend. Isn't that right Vance?" the girl rambles on at a fast pace.

"Um, yeah," Vance replies, rubbing the back of his neck, his face the color of a tomato.

"Oh, where's my manners? My name is Krissy; I live next door to Vance. Sorry that I invited myself along; I hope you don't mind?" she says, wearing hopeful smile.

"I don't mind," I reply, beginning to like the energetic little pixie of a girl.

"I don't like her, why do you?" Kylah huffs, bent out of shape.

"You guys have fun, and stay out of trouble," Jack chuckles, his eyes wrinkling at the corners.

"No shifting, Kylah," Jace says sternly.

We head outside and once the door is closed Krissy

rambles again. "Did you see how happy Jack looked? I haven't seen him that happy in over a year. How did you make him smile? Are you guys dating?"

"Woah! Slow down. No, we aren't dating; he's way too old for me. He's my guardian for now, and I don't know why he's happy," I reply, not wanting Vance to think I'm taken.

"Oh sorry. I didn't mean anything by it, just the thought of his long lost love showing up in his life to bring joy back to his bleak existence would be ever so romantic, don't you think?" she asks, her voice rising and falling dramatically with each sentence she utters.

"She always talks this much," Montoya says out of nowhere.

"Krissy, let Lia catch her bearings; this is her first time meeting you," Vance warns Krissy, his face betraying the aggravation he hides from his voice.

"I'm sorry. I don't mean to ramble on, but the world is full of beautiful things, and my brain is full of words wanting to be expressed at the sight of them," she explains, her head tilted down and eyes dropped.

"I don't mind too much," I say as I pat her on the back and draw my lips into a small smile.

"See Vance, I told you we would be the best of friends," she grins up at him, her eyes twinkling with mirth.

"Let's just go, the others are meeting us at the diner," he shakes his head; his eyes raise to the ceiling as if he's trying to keep his temper.

"Who are we meeting at the diner?" I ask, suddenly feeling self-conscious. I take a deep breath and straighten my spine.

"Vance's friends. There's Kenton, Reid, Dom, and Spence. They'll most likely ignore us, which is why I made Vance bring me along. I didn't want you to get bored with all those guys around," she answers, her inflections exaggerating each sentence. This girl should be an actress.

"I'm excited to meet your friends," I tell Vance, smiling with my eyes. Damn this boy is hot.

We load into Vance's truck, Krissy placing me in the middle. She talks the entire way to the diner, but I'm not paying attention. I'm too distracted by the proximity of my leg to Vance's. We pull up in front of a plain building with Pop's written on the sign above the door.

I remember to play the role of the girl I chose to be and follow Krissy out of the truck bravely.

"Oh, I should warn you; these guys aren't a typical group of friends. They're a mix of royal, noble, and common shifters. It's unheard of, and I'm shocked Kenton's dad hasn't made him stop," Krissy whispers, like it's a huge taboo.

"Thanks for the warning?" I say as a question, unsure of why she's telling me this.

"Leave it alone, Krissy; we are all just people who hang out. Quit trying to label people or you can go home," Vance snaps at her, his ears turning red and his lips drawn in a scowl.

"Fine, fine. I'm hungry; let's go eat," she replies, pulling on my arm.

"Wait, I don't have any money with me," I pull back, panicking for not thinking sooner.

"You don't need money; they'll just start a tab for Jack to settle at the end of the month," Vance explains patiently, giving me a small grin.

"Oh good. It worried me," I sigh, straightening my back again and following them through the door.

When my eyes adjust to the dimmer light, we're in a vintage diner you see in the movies, complete with red booths and little jukeboxes on the tables. It's nearly deserted except for a group of hot guys towards the back. Help me now; this will be interesting. I hope I don't drool.

We walk up to the circular booth the guys are sitting at,

and Vance grabs my hand and draws me to stand next to him.

"Hey guys, this is Lia. Lia, Kenton is the blonde, Reid is the redhead, Dom is the broody one with black hair, and Spence is the one with green hair," he introduces us with a huge grin.

"Nice to meet you all," I reply inspecting them closely. Kenton is built, his muscles well defined under his golden tan skin. His sapphire blue eyes sparkle above his luscious lips. Reid is much paler with bright emerald green eyes and freckles dotting his straight nose. His lips are thinner, and he has a cute dimple when he smiles. Dom has onyx eyes to match his hair, his skin a lovely mocha color, with a broad nose and full kissable lips. Finally, Spence has bright green hair with sky-blue eyes. He has a decent tan and a roman nose.

I receive a series of hellos from the guys as we sit down. They see Krissy finally and Dom groans.

"Why did you bring the chatterbox?" he growls at Vance.

"Did you want Lia to feel uncomfortable… to be the only girl with us?" Vance gives cocks his head a meets his eyes.

"I guess not," he grumbles, his face drawn in a scowl.

What is his deal? He has no right to be so rude to anyone just because they're a little different.

"You should apologize! How rude can you get! Come on Krissy, we can sit somewhere else," I exclaim, grabbing Krissy by the arm and pulling her towards the front of the diner.

"No one has ever stuck up for me like that. You really do like me," the short girl throws her arms around me in a bear hug.

"I don't agree with people being rude like that," I reply squeezing her back. "Can you let go now though? I can't breathe."

"Sorry. I'm overly excitable, I know, and it gets on

people's nerves," she explains, her eyes shining with unshed tears.

"It doesn't matter. You should be free to be yourself without buttheads judging you." I scowl.

"If you had to live with her around all the time, you would do the same," Montoya says.

"You're too nice," Kylah sighs.

Vance walks over and I glare at him. He didn't stick up for Krissy, so he's equally guilty in my book. "I'm sorry Dom wasn't nice to you Krissy; I'll still give you guys a ride home when you're done if you want. This didn't go the way I had hoped."

He walks off; his shoulders drooped, and I feel bad for him. At least he apologized.

"I'm so excited you're here to do things with. When we get to school, we'll have each other to hang out with and avoid the mean girls. There are some really mean girls in town..." Krissy drones on and I tune her out. I'm too busy watching Kenton stalking up to the table. There's something predatory in the way he moves, and I'm starting to feel as if I'm his prey.

"You're not listening to a word I'm saying are you," she accuses me, her arms crossed across her chest.

"Sorry," I mumble as Kenton reaches the table.

"He's a lion; I like him too," Kylah purrs.

"Lia, please don't judge us all by Dom's personality. He was really rude to Krissy, but you didn't give the rest of us a chance," he grins, holding out his hands to persuade us to come back to the table with him.

"If he was sorry, he would apologize to Krissy himself," I reply, dropping my chin slightly and turning my lips down into a frown.

"If he apologizes, you'll join us?" he asks, hope reverberating in his tone.

"Only if Krissy wants to," I answer, not wanting to make her sit somewhere she feels uncomfortable.

"Let's go," she squeals excitedly, jumping up from her seat and pulling me with her.

We follow Kenton back to the guys and he glares a Dom. "You have something you want to say?"

"He's a cheetah, it's hard for them to trust," Kylah whispers. *"I still like him."*

"Sorry I was rude. I'll bite my tongue next time," he growls through clenched teeth. The muscle on the side of his jaw is twitching in annoyance.

"No problem," Krissy says in her sing-song voice and smiles at him.

I sit down and slide over so Krissy can sit next to me. I keep an eye on Dom, but he has his head buried in a menu.

"What's good to eat here?" I ask, my stomach gnawing on itself.

"Everything," Spence grins over his menu at me.

"He's another tiger, and a beautiful one," Kylah keeps me informed.

"Well then, maybe I'll need to order everything," I tease, trying to decide what to eat.

"Frieda, bring out one of everything and we'll all share," Kenton yells to the woman behind the counter then turns and smiles at me.

I can't decide if my jaw should drop or I should swoon. I'm in trouble with these handsome guys around. They all seem to be good friends, so I don't need to be dating any of them. That's a recipe for trouble. I would like to have friends in this new life instead.

The food arrives and there's everything from hamburgers to mac and cheese. We all eat a bit of everything and before long the food is gone.

"I'm shocked we ate all that food," I say, leaning back and closing my eyes now that my stomach is full.

"Get used to it. We're all sixteen so it will take a lot to feed us as a group," Reid chuckles, his green eyes twinkling.

"He's a panther like us," Kylah purrs.

"What are we doing next?" I ask, unsure if this was all Vance had planned or not.

"Swimming?" Spence asks grinning.

"Swimming!" Reid exclaims, smiling ear to ear.

"Swimming it is. Lia, would you like to join us?" Kenton asks, pulling his lips up in a smile that flashes his perfect white teeth.

"I'll need to run home first and get my bathing suit," I reply, my stomach full of butterflies. I can't decide if I'm nervous or excited.

"Why do you want to swim?" Kylah asks, unable to understand why the draw to the water.

"I'm out. I don't understand how your cats can stand the water," Krissy visibly shudders.

"I'll run Krissy home if you can take Lia to Jack's?" Vance offers, staring at Kenton.

"Sure thing, if Lia is ok riding with me," Kenton replies, glancing at me for an answer.

"Let's go," I say, before I can chicken out.

"We'll meet you there," Dom mutters.

CHAPTER EIGHT

I follow Kenton outside, wondering what Dom's problem is. Maybe I shouldn't go since he doesn't want me around. Kenton walks up to a bright red Ford Mustang and my jaw drops.

"I'm Percy," Kenton's lion introduces himself.

"One of the perks of being royalty is my dad lets me drive whatever I want," he grins, his eyes crinkling at the edges.

"That's a nice perk," I agree. "Maybe you should just drop me off. I don't think Dom wants me there, and I don't want to upset anyone."

"Don't worry about Dom; he's just having a bad day, and he's mad that we stuck up for Krissy. She does talk a lot," Kenton explains, rubbing the back of his neck.

"She does, but that's no reason to be mean," I point out.

"You're right. We should all try to do better," he sighs, not taking his eyes off the road.

We pull up to the house, and I jump out to run inside; Kenton follows.

"You can wait here, I'll be fast." I feel awkward about coming home with a different guy than I left with.

"I want to say hi to Jack." He pulls the corner of his mouth up into a lopsided grin.

I shrug and go through the front door and head to my room. I go straight to my drawer and put on the two-piece bathing suit the sales lady picked out for me. It's a black string bikini top with boy shorts. I peer into the vanity and decide I like the way it fits, then pull a t-shirt and loose shorts on over and I'm ready to go.

I pull my hair up in a messy bun as I walk out of my room. Kenton and Jack are chatting on the couch in the living room when I enter.

"Be careful and take food with you." Jack's eyes darken.

"We will, Jack." Kenton flashes a smile.

I wave goodbye as we walk out the door. When we get into the car, I sit back and relax. I'm determined to have a good time regardless of why I'm here.

"Have you ever been swimming before?" Kenton glances sideways away from the road.

"Yeah. Not all cats hate water," I tilt my head down, with my brow raised, challenging him to argue.

"This will be a blast then." He laughs as he hits the accelerator, speeding up as we hit the open road.

I close my eyes and enjoy the ride. We're well outside of town when he stops the car. I open my eyes and examine the area. We're parked next to two other vehicles, one of them being Vance's truck. In front of the cars, there are large stones placed to where the cars can't drive through. A dirt path leads into the trees just beyond the large stones.

I grab my bag with a towel in it and follow Kenton down the dirt path. The trail leads under a canopy of beautiful trees and underbrush. Kylah purrs under the surface, wanting out to roam around. I mentally give her a firm no, which causes her to huff and lay down, almost pouting. I ignore her, instead focusing on following Kenton. *It's a nice view to focus on,* I think, then giggle.

"If it wouldn't make Jace mad, I could make you run," she huffs before ignoring me.

"Good thing you don't want to make him mad then," I think back at her.

"What's so funny back there?" He glances over his shoulder, with one eyebrow raised.

"Nothing, just arguing with my kitty," I spit out between giggles.

"Does she argue back?" he draws his eyebrows together in confusion.

"Doesn't yours?" I fake pout, sticking my bottom lip out for dramatic affect.

"Don't pout, Trouble," he chuckles then pivots forward and continues walking.

"Trouble?" I ask confused by what he means.

"Your new name is Trouble, because I have a feeling that is what you will be." He laughs.

"Oh," I reply, unsure of how to react. I file it away for later.

The path curves and dumps us out at the edge of a large pond fed by a waterfall. It gorgeous and the perfect temperature out to wade in the water.

The other guys are already in the water splashing around. I drop my bag and start stripping off my clothes to join them.

"See, trouble," Kenton mumbles under his breath.

I pretend like I don't hear him and run into the water determined to splash Vance. I get close enough to draw my knees up and feel a pair of strong arms grab me around the waist.

"No fair! I almost had him!" I yell in mock anger, complete with the uh at the end.

"If you almost had him, you would have seen me sneaking up behind you," Spence laughs, waggling his eyebrows at me.

"My person thinks he's always funny, my name is Tress," Spence's tiger introduces himself.

"Mine is always brooding," Kylah huffs, sniffing the air.

"You could have let me," I pout, sticking my lips out again.

"Don't tease us with those lips, Killer," Spence sighs and puts me down. "It's not fair."

"Ah leave the kitten alone, Spence. She thinks she can run with the big cats so let her," Dom sneers.

"We don't want you here. Find someone else to date," Dom's cheetah sneers.

"Back off," Kylah growls.

"I'm not looking for anyone to date, moron," I think back at him.

"What the fuck is your problem! I don't even know you to have done something to you!" I yell at him. I don't like the attitude he's had since I first laid eyes on him.

"You're the problem; waltz in here like you belong but you will destroy this group," he huffs, as he makes his way out of the water.

"How am I going to destroy this group? I just fucking met you all. It's not like I would date any of you, anyway. I'm not into making friends then losing them because of stupid shit," I growl at him, Kylah prowling for a fight.

"Really?" he asks dumbfounded, stopping in his tracks, staring at me with an expression of pure confusion.

"Well, yeah. I just moved here. I don't know anyone, and Vance is the first person I met. He was nice enough to introduce me to all of you. Why would I ruin that by trying to choose one of you to date? That's stupid," I explain, dropping my eyebrows in confusion.

"One reason I'm so nasty to Krissy is she's always trying

to get one of us to date her," Dom whispers then leaves the water and sits on a towel.

"We protect our group. No one will destroy it. My name is Victor," Dom's cheetah introduces himself.

I file that information back to think on later and go back to goofing around. After Dom and I finish our argument, the tension leaves so the rest of the afternoon flies by in a blur. My stomach audibly growls.

"You guys! We forgot to feed Trouble," Kenton hollers, making his way out of the pond.

"Who cares about her; we forgot to feed ourselves!" Reid shouts back, giving me a wink as he follows Kenton.

"He thinks he's funny. I'm his panther Wood," Reid's panther says.

I snort out loud and Reid gives me a weird look.

"I just met Wood. Reid and Wood sounded funny," I explain, shrugging my shoulders. "You know how wood-winds use reeds?"

He gives me a strange look then walks off.

I shake my head giggling and follow them to the shore. I spread out my towel and sit on one of the giant rocks that make up the shoreline and relax back on my elbows. The guys are all digging into bags and a cooler sitting two rocks over, so I figure it's easier to wait and grab whatever they leave behind.

"Here, Kitten," Dom says, tossing me a bag of chips, beef jerky, and trail mix. "If you wait for them to finish, there will be nothing left."

He sits on the rock next to me and silently hands me a bottle of water, which I accept. We sit and eat without exchanging words or even glances.

"Listen, I'm sorry. You're right. I didn't give you a fair chance, but they're my family and I don't want anyone messing with that," Dom turns and explains. "Can we start over?"

"Sounds fair. Hi, my name is Amelia, but my friends call me Lia," I reply, offering my hand for him to shake.

"Nice to meet you Lia. My name is Dominic, but my friends call me Dom," he grins, taking my hand and giving it a quick shake.

His entire face lights up when he grins. I thought he was handsome when he was scowling, but words can't describe what I'm thinking and my jaw drops.

"Everything ok?" he asks, his brows bunched in worry.

"She probably had a heart attack from seeing you smile," Kenton teases, around a mouthful of sandwich.

"That was totally it," I giggle, then take a drink of water to hide the rest of my expressions.

When we've all finished eating, we pick up the area and go back to the cars. The sun is sitting low on the horizon and I remember what I needed to do today.

"Crap I forgot to go buy cookware. Jack has nothing in his house to cook with," I say aloud, kicking myself.

"We can grab cookware and meet you at Jack's," Dom offers.

"I thought the store would be closed by the time we got back?" I reply, not sure where they'll get cookware.

"Ah, there's the benefit to your grandparents owning said store. I'll add it to Jack's tab," he grins, lighting up his entire face, his eyes shining.

"Killer's riding back with me. Dom you ride with Kenton," Spence orders, then turns to me. "Hop in."

I open the door to the black Camaro and sit down hesitantly.

"Do you all drive fancy cars?" I ask, feeling a little out of my element.

"Only those of us with noble blood," he replies, almost spitting the words out in anger.

"I take it that's a bad thing?" I ask gently, not wanting to upset my new friend.

He stays quiet, his face showing that he's trying to put words to his thoughts as we drive back towards town.

"It's not a bad thing. It affords advantages those of the common class don't have, but I don't think they should be separated like that. Just because I was born to different parents, I have more advantages than Vance or Dom. They won't be told who to marry when they get older, but I will if my tiger doesn't find his mate. I'm bad at voicing this," he admits, knuckles white from gripping the steering wheel so hard.

"I can understand what you mean. Why do you have to go somewhere and do certain things just because of who you were born to?" I sigh, lost in my own thoughts.

"Exactly!" he exclaims a grin on his face. "Killer, you and I will get along just fine."

We ride the rest of the way to Jack's house in silence. I hope he doesn't get upset I'm bringing home a houseful. Wait, I don't really care if he does or not, I realize. At least, I'm attempting to fit in.

"Should we invite Krissy over?" I ask, thinking about my new friend.

"Please don't. I don't want to have to listen to Dom complain about her flirting all evening," Spence begs, wincing at the thought.

"Ok, I feel guilty that we basically ditched her." I stare at my feet.

"Don't feel too bad. Once she sees you won't set her up with any of us, she'll disappear soon enough," he growls. "Crap, I didn't mean to say that out loud."

"Too late. Do you really think that's why she wants to be my friend?" I ask, unsure if I should trust this information.

"She's always trying to get one of the boys," Tress growls.

"Call her tonight and tell her you only want to hang out away from us and see what she says," he replies, lifting one side of his mouth trying to soften the blow.

"I'll do that. Thank you for being honest with me, Spence," I reply, bumping his shoulder with mine.

"Anytime, Killer," he grins as we pull up in front of Jack's house.

Vance and Reid arrive directly behind us. I run up to the front door and it opens as I reach for the doorknob. Jack drops his eyebrows as he takes in the guys.

"I was going to see what you wanted me to order, but maybe we should eat out," he says, sounding overwhelmed.

"No need, Dom went to go get cookware, and we'll make dinner here. If you'll excuse me, I need to get cleaned up," I say as I push my way around him and make a beeline to my room. I grab yoga pants and a t-shirt and pop in the bath-room for a quick shower.

CHAPTER NINE

*W*hen I come back into the living room, the guys are cooking already, Jack included.

"Wow! I figured I would be the one cooking for you guys!" I exclaim, shocked at the sight.

"When you get to be this hungry, you learn to cook quickly. Except for Jack, he's the weird one," Reid replies, elbowing Jack in the ribs while he speaks.

"Hey now. I can cook; I just don't like to," Jack says defensively, clutching his chest dramatically.

"What are we eating?" I ask thinking I smell tomato sauce.

"Spaghetti. It's the only thing that will feed a group of cats this large," Dom answers as if it's obvious.

"Set the table, dinner is almost ready," Jack orders just as the sauce bubbles and pops all over his shirt.

"Aye, aye captain," I reply while laughing.

He leaves to go change his shirt, and I get plates out for everyone. I search for a chair since the table only seats six and we have seven people. While I'm busy trying to figure out what to do, Jack comes back with an extra bar stool.

"It would have been nice to know you had an extra seat," I

tease him; the corners of my mouth turned up in a slight smile.

"Dig in," Reid calls from the kitchen.

I grab a plate and dart to the food to get mine first. I remember Dom's warning at the pond and don't want to take any chances.

"Looks like she learned your numbers fast, boys," Jack grabs his sides laughing.

We sit down and eat huge plates of spaghetti and garlic bread while the guys regale me of stories from when they were younger. It's clear that this group is super close and have been for a long time. I have mixed feelings right now. Glad that they're including me but also like I'm standing on the outside looking in.

"Quit looking so serious, Jet," Reid bumps me with his shoulder, bringing me out of my thoughts.

"Sorry, just thinking of school starting up," I reply, giving a half-truth.

"It will be crazy. They require cats from all over the world to come here for those years. I mean you know, that's why you're staying with Jack," Kenton speaks animatedly, his face lighting up with excitement.

"That's what makes me nervous. You've all known each other forever, and I'm starting out new," I reply biting my lower lip nervously.

"You have us now, Kitten," Dom replies, staring at me like he can see in my soul.

"That makes me luckier than most," I reply with a small smile, still nervous they'll ditch me as soon as school starts.

"It does. Now, let's get this mess cleaned up," Jack says clapping his hands together for emphasis.

I pick my plate up, but it's grabbed in a whirlwind of action before I have time to say a word about it. I sit and watch the guys clean up like a well-oiled machine, without even saying a word to each other.

"We need to get going, but it was fun hanging out. Can we exchange numbers?" Kenton asks, grinning like the cat that got the milk.

"Sure? Vance already has my number," I reply, taking my phone out and unlocking it.

Reid plucks it from my hand and starts programing phone numbers in, while Vance texts my number to the rest of them. He hands me my phone back and we say our goodbyes.

Once everyone leaves, I sit on the couch and start playing on my phone. I survey the contacts and start giggling. Reid has named them all silly things, so I don't have a clue who is who. I look at my previous text messages and figure out Vance is 'Wannabe Farm Boy.' Now I need to figure out who 'Teen Spirit', 'Ungodly Handsome', 'Eeyore', and 'Bush' are. I'm fairly sure I know who each is, but I'll wait until tomorrow to ask.

"So, you made fast friends with an interesting bunch," Jack speaks up beside me. I forgot he was sitting there so I jump and grab my chest.

"Is that a bad thing? I'm trying to fit in and make the most of things," I say challenging him to contradict me.

"Not saying it's a bad thing, just strange. Those boys have been a tight-knit group since they met when they were tiny. They don't let people in easily is all. I'm friends with Kenton's brother so they've been underfoot as long as I can remember," he explains, trying to calm my raised hackles.

"Oh, I forgot I need to text Krissy!" I exclaim, changing the subject.

I don't know why you bother. Cat's don't lie, Kylah bites out.

I walk off to my bedroom texting her on the way.

Me: Sorry you didn't want to go swimming. Maybe we can hang out tomorrow.

Krissy: You hanging out with the guys again?

Me: No, I thought it could just be you and me.

Krissy: Oh, no, sorry. I'm busy.

Me: Ok. Let me know when you'd want to hang out then. I know the guys don't really want to hang out with all of us, but I'd like to hang out with you still.

I waited for about ten minutes and never received a response. Spence was right. I try not to let it bother me, but I get pissed off that she tried to be my friend to use me. I hate fake people. There's a knock on my door.

"Come in," I call out.

"I meant to tell you, they delivered your school uniforms today," Jack says, coming in and sitting on my bed.

"Why are girls so hard to understand," I huff, drawing my knees up to my chest, pulling my eyes open wide, trying to prevent the hot tears from escaping.

"I guess Krissy wasn't interested in you at all?" Jack asks, awkwardly patting my back. "I don't know how to do this emotional stuff, but I'm glad someone clued you in about her sooner rather than later."

"I know. I'm more mad than sad. I just don't enjoy being new and not knowing things, and I don't like people trying to use me," I growl between clenched teeth; the tears falling despite my attempt at holding them back.

"Those guys will not mess with you. What you see is what you get, though I'm shocked Dom wasn't scowling at you. If you're on his good side, they'll have your back," Jack explains giving me a tentative smile.

"I hope that's true. They've been a great bunch of guys so far," I sigh, standing up to go check out the uniforms.

I open the closet and on the side that was previously

empty is a collection of black and grey dresses, tops, skirts, and pants.

"No color allowed?" I ask, turning my nose up.

"They have an image to maintain," Jack shrugs. "You can add color with accessories and makeup. That's why your haircut is brilliant."

"I'm glad I took the risk. I need clippers to keep it short though," I reply while going through the closet, shaking my head at the lack of color.

"There's an open house tomorrow. We can go up and you can see your room and leave anything you won't need the next few days there," Jack mentions, wringing his hands together while he speaks.

"Sounds good. It'll be nice to know where to go when I get there officially," I respond, relieved that I had the chance to get the lay of the land ahead of time.

"You can see if the guys want to come along," Jack suggests as he stands up and leaves the room.

I get my phone out and text Vance.

Me: Jack is taking me up to Nightfall Academy for orientation, you guys want to come?

Vance: Sure, let me add the others in a group text.

Me: Can they say their names so I can change them in my phone?

Ungodly Handsome: Don't you like the nicknames?

Me: I would like them better if I knew who was who to start with.

Bush: What's my nickname, this is Spence.

Me: Bush, lol.

Spence: Butthead.

Teen Spirit: This is Kenton, should I even ask?

Me: Teen Spirit

Kenton: Why?

Ungodly Handsome: because it sounded fun at the time.

Eeyore: This is Dom, and what did Reid make his own?

Me: You are Eeyore and Reid called himself Ungodly Handsome.

Kenton: Reid, why confuse the poor girl, now was there a reason for this chat besides figuring out who we are?

Vance: Oh yeah! Lia invited us to go to orientation with her tomorrow.

Reid: I'm down.

Dom: See you then.

Spence: You don't even have to ask, Killer.

Kenton: Meet you at Jack's. Text us the time.

Me: See you guys tomorrow.

I put the phone down and smile ear to ear. Maybe this new life won't be so bad. I get my luggage out and start packing the school uniforms and other things I think I can go without. When I finish, I lay down without bothering to change clothes.

KNOCK. Knock. Knock,

"What!" I snap, wanting to go back to sleep.

"There are five boys in the living room that woke me up knocking, so you're getting your butt out of bed too!" Jack growls, puffy bags appearing under his eyes.

I crawl out of bed and follow him to the living room, and they're all sitting there wearing sheepish expressions.

"You never told us what time, so we picked one," Reid grins, while shrugging his shoulders.

"Next time call first," I growl, but soften it with my eyes. "Since you're here, do you want to go for a run?"

"In human form," Jack barks.

"That's what I meant." I roll my eyes.

"He's no fun. I tried to get him to let us run as cats," Kylah sighs.

The guys laugh, so I figure they had other plans like my panther.

"I'm not allowed to shift until after we go through training at Nightfall either," Kenton whispers in my ear. "My lion has a strong personality."

"I can relate." I smile shyly, unsure of how much I should share. I pull my sneakers on and head towards the door. "You guys coming?"

The guys slowly start to follow as Jack puts on his shoes. "Guess I could do with a run."

"You don't trust us?" Spence asks, gasping, dropping his jaw, and holding his chest in mock defense.

"Not in the slightest," Jack replies, winking at me.

We take off down a trail in the back of the house, but in a different way than we had ran previously. It feels good to let my muscles loose and just run, but Kylah is prowling under the surface threatening to break free. The pressure builds and builds, so I stop running.

"Sorry, but I need to run, sister," she says then runs towards the surface.

"Jack..." I say as my panther explodes out.

"I was afraid of this," he sighs and lets Jace free.

Almost as if it's a chain reaction the guys all shift. I see that Kenton is a gorgeous lion with a vibrant mane and that has the power backing of an alpha. He's huge next to the rest of us. Spence is a tiger shifter with vibrant stripes and still twice the size of me, but he doesn't feel dominant at all. Vance is a tiger, but not as big or vibrant as Spence. Dom is a cheetah shifter who's smaller than me. Finally, Reid is a black panther like me, only he has a white toe on his front paw. It's still strange seeing the world through my panther eyes.

Jack herds us back the way we came, and we run the trail

that I ran shifted. Kylah is content to run and let me stay in control with this many cats around, which makes it freeing. When we arrive in the grove, she is insistent we climb, and Reid chases us up the closest tree. Kylah really likes all the guys and their cats, so she feels comfortable enough to let her guard down and play.

We chase each other back and forth until she is exhausted and content. I shift back without meaning to.

"I'm going back to the house. See you all there!" I exclaim and take off running, buck-naked back to the house.

Dom and Jack pass me in cat form, so I glance over my shoulder and the other guys have shifted back. I'm not supposed to have issues with nudity in shifter society, but for the first time I feel self-conscious. I run harder and head straight to my room when I arrive at the house. I grab clothes, jump in the shower, and get ready for the day.

Once I'm dressed with my hair done and makeup in place, I feel ready to face the guys again. I hated the thought of the routine when it was given to me, but now it's oddly comforting. I walk out to the living room and the guys are all dressed like nothing ever happened. They must keep spare clothes with them just in case something like this happens. That's a good idea and something I should do as well.

"Let's go out and get breakfast," Jack suggests, staring at me hard like he's afraid of a reaction.

"Sounds great to me! I'm hungry," I reply excited to eat.

"Before we go, I have a question," Kenton speaks up, wringing his hands nervously. "Where's your white spot, Trouble?"

"That's a bit rude don't you think?" Jack interrupts before I'm able to answer.

"No, I think if we are bringing her into our circle then secrets don't make friends. What's wrong, you suddenly don't trust us?" Kenton pushes out his chest his face turning red, and his eyes narrowing.

"I trust you, but you're asking her to trust you with her very life the day after she met you," Jack meets him with an equally aggressive stance staring him in the eye.

"We can trust them. I'll tell Jack to back off," Kylah says, her tail flicking in irritation.

"Don't fight. If I have to shift at school, people will figure it out anyway. I didn't know I had to fabricate a hard to see white spot. I don't have one Kenton, just like you noticed," I replied, staring him in the eye, daring him to make a big deal out of it.

"Don't worry, we'll help you keep your secret. I know you don't know us and have no reason to trust us, but we'll help you come up with some white hair somewhere," Spence grabs my hands and kneels.

"Either way, it's easier to get this conversation out of the way now and not at school. Can we go eat now?" I ask grinning, trying to diffuse the suddenly awkward tension in the room.

"Trouble's riding with me since I caused this mess!" Kenton shouts and grabs my hand, pulling me towards his car.

I giggle and follow so not to trip and hop in the passenger seat.

"I'm sorry Lia. I should have thought that through before I just blurted it out," he says once he shuts the car door.

"You would have found out eventually." I shrug, playing it off as if it doesn't bother me.

He glances at me from the side of his eye then opens his mouth but closes it again. Instead, he just starts the car and we return to the cafe we ate at yesterday. I jump out as soon as the wheels stop turning and go straight inside, my stomach leading the way. They sit there awkwardly silent all staring at the menu, trying to avoid any direct eye contact.

"Ok, this awkward crap has got to stop. I don't care about how things went down. If you can look past it, I can too." I clap my hands together, causing half the table to jump.

"All right, Killer. We'll behave." Spence nudges me in the ribs while grinning.

After that everyone chats until the food arrives then we're so busy stuffing our faces there's no room for talking. When we finish eating, we go back to Jack's house. I ride with Kenton again, but we're quiet the entire way.

"I think now is the time to really explain what is going on, so everyone knows the real stakes," Jack announces staring at me with concern in his eyes.

"I take it there's more that you haven't told me?" I ask, chewing on my lip.

"So, I told you about what happened to my brother?" he asks, and I nod my head. "The reason there are royal panther girls hidden is because of a prophecy. There's a group that wants to kill all the female panthers born around your age. Even some that had minimal white on them."

"So, there are people out there that want to kill me?" I ask clenching my fists so tight my nails are leaving marks on my palms. I file the prophecy away for later and make a note to ask him about it when I grasp the rest of this.

"We don't know. The last reported activity from that group was right after my brother..." Jack trails off his eyes glazing over, lost in thought. "On any account, if any of you decide to out her, you are possibly putting a bounty on her head."

"I won't do anything to hurt you, Trouble."

"Me either, Killer."

"You can count on me, Kitten."

"What's with all these nicknames?" Jack asks raising one eyebrow.

"They seem to fit her. Isn't that right, Jet?" Reid teases me.

"Sorry Lia, I haven't thought of one." Vance shrugs. "Is it time to go to orientation and forget all this serious crap?"

"Sounds good to me, let me grab my bag," I reply, ready to avoid thinking about the bomb Jack just dropped. I'll question him later to get the full story, but I'm not ready for that yet.

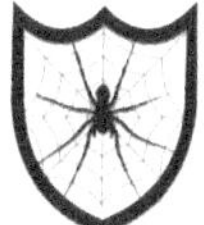

CHAPTER TEN

"*L*et's take two cars," Jack tells the guys as I leave the room.

I arrive back with my bag, and they had separated into two groups already.

"You're with me," Jack waves his hand over and takes my bag.

"Why is the school so secluded?" I ask as we walk out to the car.

"I'm honestly not sure," Jack answers as he places my bag in the trunk.

Vance and Dom follow behind, placing their bags with mine. I sit in the front while they scrunch in the back. We take off, Kenton follows with Reid and Spence in tow.

"Have either of you ever been to the Academy before?" I ask the guys in the backseat.

"Nope; no one is allowed to go until orientation day," Vance explains.

"That's strange don't you think?" I ask, puzzled on why all the strange rules.

"It's always been that way," Jack shrugs not taking his eyes off the road.

We drive for a while then pass under a large stone arch with a giant spider on it. I stare with my jaw gaping wide open.

"Why the heck is there a giant spider on that arch?" I ask freaking out internally.

"That's the symbol of the Huntsman clan. I forgot you didn't grow up in the clan. It's some heavy shit to find out today," Vance answers staring at his feet.

"If you guys don't want to hang out with me because of it, that's ok," I tell them, feeling rejected.

"Oh no! I just feel bad that we outed a huge secret on accident, and you didn't get the chance to tell us in your own time," he assures me, putting his hand on my shoulder.

"I'm ok with you knowing. Besides, it allowed me to learn that I don't know enough about my own situation," I reply staring daggers at Jack.

"Hey, I was going to tell you eventually. I was trying not to overload you all at once," he says defensively, the tips of his ears turning crimson.

"Let's talk about this later and focus on this school thing. The building looks creepy to me," I say staring out the front window at the large dark stone building looming in front of us.

"Home," Kylah purrs, excited to see the school.

The remote location, paired with the dark stone and spiders, gives it a creepy ominous feel. Hopefully, that goes away once we get inside.

"It's better inside, I promise," Jack assures me, using his gift no doubt.

We park in the tiny parking lot and unload from the car. Kenton pulls up beside us shortly after. We all grab our bags and follow Jack to the front door. I feel hesitant, but my companions appear to be excited. When we approach the door, the man from the airport is waiting; his eyebrows raised in surprise at the group.

"You've made fast friends with an interesting bunch, Amelia," he says, drawing my name out into four syllables.

"Just trying to fit in, Sir," I reply, remembering not to stare him in the eye.

"It appears like you remembered something. Very well, I'm sure Jack can show you all around, and the staff is around if you have any questions," he says then slinks off.

"My dad said he was creepy, but I didn't realize how much until now," Spence whispers in my ear.

It takes everything in me not to giggle, but there was no way I want to draw Sir's attention back to me.

"Let's start with the dorms so we can drop off your stuff. We'll get your keys from the dorm master," Jack says, taking on an air of authority in his voice.

"Yes Sir," Reid says, saluting him, lips turned up in a wide smile.

"You guys know that Sir takes his Sir very seriously right?" I ask them, causing Reid to pale a bit. "Please lead the way, Jack."

"Thank you, Amelia. Now, all your classes will be in the west wing and the dorms are situated in the east wing. They are separated by class; common dorms are on the first floor, noble dorms are on the second floor, and royal are on the third," he explains as we walk.

"Where am I going to be?" I ask, suddenly self-conscious.

"That's a good question. It's wherever the panther queen placed you," Jack gives me a nervous smile.

"What if she places me on the royal floor?" I whisper, freaking out.

"That could make it easier to hide in plain sight. Some royal children are sent off as young children to learn elsewhere. We would just have to work hard on getting your politics caught up before school starts," he whispers back, the other guys all leaning in to listen.

"I guess we'll find out soon," I reply, finally bringing my attention to my surroundings.

The walls inside are still stone but a much lighter color. The ceiling is high, there are tapestries of different cat shifters every so often, and paintings of various men and women.

We approach a large staircase and head up to the first floor. There's a large, dark mahogany wood desk as we exit the stairs with hallways branching off in either direction from it.

"Hello dears, I'm Ms. Blackburn the dorm master, can I have your names to find your rooms?" A kind, dark-haired woman asks. She's tall and thin with grey eyes and deep smile lines.

"We have Vance Avery, Dominic Perrie, Spencer Williams, Reid Thielman, Kenton Huntsman, and Amelia Huntsman," Jack lists off our names.

"Give me a few minutes, and I'll get you all sorted," she replies as she shuffles through a stack of paperwork.

After finding each person's paperwork, she gets on her computer then produces a key card for each of us with our names and room numbers written on them.

"These are your student IDs, don't lose them," she explains in a stern voice, the crinkle of her eyes betraying her smile.

"Yes ma'am, thank you for helping us," Kenton responds flashing her an award-winning smile.

"Now, Avery and Perrie, you're on this floor to the right. Williams and Thielman, you're on the second floor to the right. Finally, Amelia you're on the left, and Kenton you're on the right on the top floor. Here's a list of dorm rules. Have a nice day," she smiles as she hands us each a packet of paperwork.

We split up, Dom and Vance taking the hallway to the right of the desk, the rest of us heading up the stairs. At the next landing, we lose Reid and Spence; the three of us who are left continuing up.

"I should stay in good shape living up here," I comment offhandedly.

"I agree; I wish we weren't separated like this," Kenton replies his eyes turned down.

"I'm sure there are plenty of places to hang out regardless," I try to reassure him. "There's a whole packet of rules to dictate it."

He turns up one corner of his mouth in half a smile, "At least I can walk you down every morning."

I shake my head with a small smile as we reach the top landing. I turn left while Kenton turns right, and Jack stands there hesitating.

"Are you waiting there? Or..." I ask Jack confused why he's stood there.

"I wasn't sure if you wanted me following you," he rubs his hand on the back of his neck.

"I'd rather have company, and you are my guardian," I reply, hoping he follows me.

I glance down at my key card, and it has the number one on it. There are only ten rooms on this hallway and a good distance between each door. I'm thankful my door is right off the stairs. I use the key card and the room is huge. The furniture I picked out is already taking up the area that was clearly made for the bedroom. I need a desk and sitting room furniture to fill out the room.

"Sorry, I honestly didn't know what all you would need. We can go to the furniture store and see what they have that will work after this," Jack says, his lips scrunched to the side, a look of concentration covers his face as he examines the empty space.

There are two doors off to the right side of the room, I open the first and it's a huge closet. I set my suitcase down and start unpacking my uniforms and what street clothes I brought, and the closet seems empty still. I sigh and make a mental note not to let anyone see how bare it is. The next door is a private bathroom with a nice tub and shower. This was the part I worried about the most, sharing a shower with a group of girls.

"So, this is how the top floor lives," Jack says with amusement in his voice.

"How was your floor?" I ask, curious what it'll be like for everyone else.

"On the noble floor, you have your own rooms that are roughly the size of the bedroom portion with a bathroom shared to the room next door. The common floor they share two to a room and four bathrooms to the hall," he replies like it's normal.

"That's horrible. There shouldn't be such a separation," I reply, then feel guilty that I'm glad to be at the top.

"Don't feel guilty. You didn't even ask for this life or any of this stuff. Let it be compensation for how everything else went down," Jack hugs me rubbing my back.

"I needed that hug, thank you," I reply, genuinely feeling better at the small gesture.

He releases me from the hug then grabs my suitcase and walks towards the door. "I bet the boys are waiting on us by now. Ready to see the rest of the school?"

"Sure, why not," I shrug and follow him.

"We can go back to LA tomorrow and get more clothes," he says bumping my shoulder when I catch up to him.

"Oh, and stuff to decorate with?" I ask, excited about personalizing the space I'll live in.

"Anything you want," he smiles, his eyes crinkling with a faint sparkle. "I think having you here will be good for me."

"Glad to be of service," I roll my eyes, but break down giggling.

When we exit the door, Kenton is standing there staring at his shoes.

"What's up buttercup?" I ask, thinking of his lion's mane.

"Just waiting on a slow princess to finish checking out her room. Are you ready, Trouble?" he asks, then winks at me.

"Let's go see what else this place has to offer us," I answer heading down the stairs.

No one is at the next landing, so we proceed past and find the rest of the group chatting with Ms. Blackburn.

"Thank you, Ms. Blackburn," Vance says as we walk up.

"No need to be so formal, call me Sarah," she replies, blushing.

"We'll see you next week," he tells her then turns to us. "Did you get lost in your fancy, dancy rooms?"

"Yup, they were so big I fell in the bathtub and Trouble had to come fish me out," Kenton replies, punching him on the shoulder.

"Quit fooling around." Jack knocks their heads together while rolling his eyes in an overly exaggerated way." Let's show you the auditorium since you have to go there, and the cafeteria since you'll be spending most of your time wishing you were there."

"Whatever you say, boss man," Spence, laughs as he walks up next to me and casually drapes his arm over my shoulder.

I like the way it feels there and no one else seems a bit bothered by it, so I let it stay. Wondering what it would feel like if I actually had a boyfriend who would do that.

"Cat alert nine o'clock," Dom whispers.

I glance up and see a girl with enormous blonde hair, a

second girl with black hair that isn't quite so overdone, and Krissy trailing their heels.

"I thought you said you weren't doing anything with them today," Krissy walks up and demands.

"Nice to see you too, and no, I offered to go do something without them to get to know you," I reply, turning back to the group.

"You should have specified," she grumps, crossing her arms over her chest.

"Maybe you should have been interested in me for me," I throw back at her while she walks back to stand by two girls I haven't met yet.

"Who's with you, Kenton? Krissy said you guys met with a new girl, but I thought she was just telling stories," the blonde girl asks, acting as if the entire world owes her an explanation.

"Hi, I'm Amelia, nice to meet you," I walk forward and hold my hand out to shake.

"No one ever taught you to respect your betters? I can't believe you just addressed me like you were allowed to. Even Krissy knows better," she sticks her nose up and raises her hand as if she will smack me.

"We should make her hurt," Kylah growls, rumbling deep in her chest.

Jack jumps up and walks in front of me, "Maybe you should check your lessons again, Amy. I don't believe that royals have ever had to hold their tongue to a noble. If you would like, I'd be happy to go research how you should be punished."

"Come on, Amy. We'll figure out more later," the dark-haired girl tugs on her hand, leading her towards the stairs.

"I have questions," I say, my eyes darting from face to face, including Spence who no longer has his arm around my shoulder.

"We can have an answer session over food. Let's get this tour over first," Jack decides, pushing us forward. "Now this is the ground floor, then you have the subfloor below us and first, second, and the third above us."

"Why is there a ground, that's weird? Shouldn't it be called the first floor?" Vance speaks up.

"Generations of Nightfall Students have asked the same thing, and no one has gotten an answer," Jack chuckles as we follow him.

We make our way to the auditorium. It's behind two immense doors in the middle of the ground floor. There is a large stage surrounded by theater seating complete with a balcony.

"There will be so many people here," I gasp.

"The balcony is only full when parents come up." Jack shrugs while turning the corners of his mouth up into a small grin.

"Food, show me where the food is. I beg you." Reid drops to his knees hands clasped together in front of Jack.

"Let's go eat lunch, you bunch of heathens," Jack sighs, throwing his hands in the air chuckling.

"You're enjoying this. Admit it," I say poking him in the ribs with my index finger.

"I am Lia. I really am," he agrees, slinging his arm over my shoulder leading me towards the stairs.

I take a moment to notice how different it feels with Jack and Spence. Jack feels like family already even though that weirds me out in a different way, but Spence feels like putting kindling on a new fire. I shake my head, pushing those thoughts away with the prospect of food. We go down the stairs to what Jack calls the sublevel, and it exits into a giant cafeteria. There are stations set up all over the room boasting original foods. They take the lunch game serious here. My stomach verbalizes my hunger and I take off to the first station. Everything smells so good.

The cook explains to me how each station makes a different food for the day. One station will focus on pizza and another on Chinese or Italian. I nod my head as I'm listening, but I just want to sit to eat what she's placed on my plate. The pizza smells amazing.

We finally break free from the line to sit and eat. I make a stop at each station before I'm satisfied.

"She's going to be powerful," Dom says around a bite of food. "Look at how much she already out eats us all."

"What do you mean?" I ask, my forehead knitting together.

" The stronger the power, the higher the appetite. Eat up." Jack grins.

"Not sure if I should be happy or freaked out," I mumble crossing my arms across my chest.

"I say embrace it. Not going to change either way." Spence grins, his green hair falling to one side.

He was right. I'm here, and that isn't changing anytime soon, so it is time to adapt. "Well then, I say I need more clothes if I'm going to keep up with the girls at this school. Can we go shopping now?" I beg Jack, in an annoying voice.

"It's like I have a little sister of my very own," he rubs the top of my head as he stands up.

He puts his dishes away and heads for the stairs. The rest of us scramble to catch up. Once we're in the car, he flashes me a grin and peels off out of the parking lot. I laugh at his playful side, which is starting to come out. Somehow, my panther has decided he is family, and that's just how it will be from now on. She purrs contentedly when she learns I've come to this realization.

"Is it normal for your cat to pick your family?" I ask, wondering if she's unique.

"He's our brother. It took you long enough to figure it out," she laughs at me.

"Tell me next time so I know," I sigh, so confused at every-thing being thrown at me.

"It's totally normal. Most cats pick their husbands when they're in school at Nightfall," Vance explains smiling.

"I mean Kylah has labelled Jack as our brother in this short time," I explain burying my head in my hands in embarrassment. I feel lost at not knowing what they grew up learning.

"Don't ever be embarrassed by who your cat chooses for what. Your cat knows best," Dom raises my head and gazes into my eyes. "The guys here? Our cats decided we were brothers when we were young."

"I didn't meet Kylah until my first shift," I say, wondering why they met theirs sooner.

"We didn't either, but our parents recognized the bond," he explains.

"It doesn't happen often, but when it does, it's some of the strongest bonds in our world, and Jace agrees that you're our sister," Jack says, his eyes crinkling in a genuine smile.

"Our family is important in keeping us safe. Not all cats have a family; we are lucky," Jace explains.

"At least we have each other," Kylah agrees.

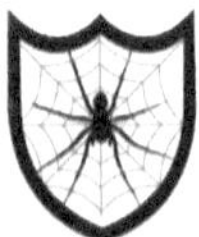

CHAPTER ELEVEN

I sit back in the seat feeling content for the first time since my birthday. Maybe everything will be ok and work itself out. I close my eyes for a second and then pop awake when we stop. I fell asleep!

"Are we really going shopping now?" I squeal getting out of the car when I see we're at the airport.

"Your wish is my command," Jack gets out of the car and bows towards the plane.

Dom, Vance, and Reid follow us to the plane.

"You guys are coming too?" I ask my eyes wide with shock.

"Duh, Kenton and Spence will be here any second. We want to get off the island too, Jet," Reid replies, bumping my shoulder with his.

As he finishes speaking, Kenton pulls up, they hop out of the car, and jog over to us.

"Besides Killer wanting clothes, what are we doing?" Spence asks the group, shoving his hands in his front pockets.

"I don't want just clothes. I need to decorate the room; it's bare," I explain.

"Hey, did you all look at the rules? Are we going to make Prince Kenton's room our hang out?" Vance asks, smirking.

"We can read it on the plane, let's go," Kenton throws the packet at Vance then walks towards the plane.

We load up on the plane and choose our seats. I sit next to a window and daydream while the guys talk about the rules. I'm feeling strange about my current circumstances. On one hand, I feel guilty for accepting the Huntsman clan as home, but the other side of me feels relief that I don't have to worry about not fitting in.

As soon as we land, I rush off the plane and take a second to call my mom.

"Everything ok, Amelia?" Mom asks, a hit of worry in her tone.

"Yes, I just need, well... is it ok that my panther, Kylah, and I feel at home here this quick?" I ask, worried what her response will be.

"That makes my heart light to hear sweetie. I've been worried sick on how well you'll fit in. If your panther has recognized it as your home already, I know you'll be fine," she gushes, pride radiating from her voice making me feel truly at peace.

"Thank you, Mom. I have to run, but I will call you again soon," I squeal hanging up the phone before she answers.

The guys were standing a short distance away giving me the illusion of privacy, though I know they could hear everything. My own hearing has been improving daily since my first shift.

"Do you feel less guilty now?" Jack asks, putting his arm around my shoulder.

"I do. I'm ready to give this a go now," I reply leaning into him, letting Kylah's purr soothe me.

We get into a waiting limo and go back to the area of town where I went shopping the first time.

"Are we going back to the same store?" I ask Jack, excited to see the sales lady again.

"Yes, I called ahead and had her grab you some choices to add to your wardrobe while you were talking to your mom," he replies, smiling at me.

"Good, then I won't make you wait too long," I reply excited to embrace the day.

The day flies by going from clothes shops to picking out stuff for all our rooms. Evening hits and we're starving, so we hit a buffet to avoid standing out among the humans as easily. It wouldn't be very normal for us to eat so much if we were just at a regular restaurant. When we've eaten our fill, it's time to go back to the plane and head home for the night.

"I'm actually excited about starting school for the first time," I admit as we board the plane.

"Me too, Kitten," Dom whispers behind me, making me jump and my panther growl audibly. "Sorry, I didn't realize how dominant your panther has already gotten."

Everyone averts their eyes, and she settles down in the back of my head again.

"What the hell was that?" I ask, a little worried about how forceful she was.

"When they say you're royal, you're a princess, Princess," Vance answers; his eyes fixed just below my nose.

"There's no way. I mean, how?" I ask falling back on the seat in the plane.

"We don't know who your biological mom is, and there are rumors that three of the panther princesses hid babies, but it was all just rumors," Kenton answers, trying to calm me down.

I feel panic racing through my veins stirring Kylah again. She paces back and forth wanting to take over and save me from myself. I try to hold back the feeling to shift but it's overwhelming.

"I need out," she hisses.

"Please, no," I beg.

"Kenton, your lion is the only cat at this point that has a chance of dominating her panther. Don't let her shift!" Jack exclaims, panic tingeing his voice and clear on his face.

"You will not shift," Percy booms.

Kenton stands in front of me his eyes partially shifting.

Kylah pauses and listens, tilting her head, trying to decide if she wants to listen to him. I beg her to please listen and assure her I'll calm down, so she huffs and lays down again not happy about it.

"I'm not dominant enough, but she paused and chose to listen," Kenton whispers, fear tingeing his voice.

"Let's not speak of this. You guys will learn to control your cats soon, so it won't be a big deal. No one can know," Jack commands, staring everyone but Kenton and myself in the eye.

"What happens when someone figures it out?" I ask, a warble betraying the nervousness I feel.

"I don't know, and that bothers me. I don't like not knowing things. We need to catch you up on how our royalty works since you will most likely become queen someday," Jack sighs, holding the sides of his hair with his hands.

"I can start with the basics. I've been learning them since I could walk," Kenton volunteers, trying to ease the nerves we can all feel radiating off Jack. "You already know about the class structure. In the royal class there are four queens. Each queen is chosen, from the royal class, by how dominant her cat is. Occasionally, the nobles have a contender because of an especially dominant cat. The lion, panther, leopard, and tiger shifters are the ruling lines. Every ten years, all the dominant princesses come together to compete for the crown. In theory, we could have one queen if one cat out dominates everyone else, but that is just an ancient prophecy."

"So, you're saying once I finish school, I will start going up every ten years to see if I can be a queen or not?" I ask not understanding the point.

"Nope, you just go up once unless you become queen. Queens are the only ones that have to come back more than once," Reid answers around a mouthful on peanuts he's eating.

"That doesn't sound so bad. What's this prophecy, Jack mentioned this before?" I ask changing the subject, trying to wrap my head around the fact that my cat is dominant enough to compete to be queen.

"Let's talk about that at home, please?" Jack asks, his hands now resting on the armrest.

We arrive at the airport shortly after, and the guys decided to go back to the house with us. I'm a bundle of nervous energy wondering why Jack wants to be at home to talk about this prophecy. I quickly unload my packages before I find myself in the kitchen, pulling out snacks for everyone.

Once everyone is sitting at the table eating, I bring up the prophecy again. "So now that we're here, are you going to explain this prophecy to the new girl?"

"This is a big deal in this clan, but we don't speak of it in the general shifter population," Kenton explains, opening his mouth to continue but Jack touches his arm.

"The reason the cats only have queens and are the only ruling branch of the shifter community goes back thousands of years to a prophecy from a gifted seer. One queen will unite the thrones when darkness falls. She will have five kings, class unseen. The strongest will bow, though many will compete, she alone will triumph as queen," Jack recites from memory.

"That is so vague why would anyone worry about it?" I ask confused.

"Five hundred years ago, a different seer saw a female panther shifter of royal blood, who will rule us all. That's why shifter princesses started having accidents regularly as babies," Kenton says, staring at his feet.

"That's why my birth mom hid me in the first place, so if anyone learns that I was adopted they might jump to conclusions." I shriek, not wanting to accept the weight of this prophecy on my shoulders. I hope there aren't still people trying to get rid of black panther princesses.

"There was a group that was devoted to keeping the society from becoming a monarchy, but they've gone silent the past fifteen years," Jack whispers, his skin pale white.

"Why are you so scared?" I whisper back around a lump in my throat.

"Because, you're the only family I have now. I can't lose you too," he admits staring at the plate sitting in front of him.

"You're my family too," I reply.

I get up and throw my arms around him, hating the pain I see on his face. Tears stream down my face when I realize as far as my panther is concerned, he's the only family I have. I hold him silently crying for what seems like ages until a pair of strong arms remove me and hug me back.

"We'll make sure you're ok. You have a loyal group. Still not sure how you weaseled in with them, but they will keep you safe," Jack says then kisses my forehead and hugs me tighter.

After our emotional moment, the evening winds down, and the guys go home. I put everything away, rush through my night routine, and fall into a restless sleep full of dreams of people trying to kill me.

CHAPTER TWELVE

The rest of the week flies by hanging out with the guys and Jack, and before I know it, it's time to move into Nightfall. I examine my room that is packed up and ready to go, and although I've only been here a week, I already know I will miss it. I close the door and sigh. The next part is even harder; time to say goodbye to Jack.

"I'm really sad I won't get to run with you every morning," I sob throwing my arms around his neck.

"I'll see you at Thanksgiving. Time will fly by," he hugs me back chuckling. "Do you have everything packed and ready to go?"

"I do, and Vance is bringing his truck to pick up everything," I reply removing myself from the hug and wiping at my eyes.

"You can text me whenever you want. Now, go and enjoy yourself," he says, pushing me back and giving me a smile.

Vance pulls up just as we finish up and comes in the house to help me load up the rest of me belongings. After they say goodbye, we hop in his truck and are off to Nightfall.

"Are you nervous?" I ask, chewing on my lip.

"Nope, I have the guys and you. What's making you so nervous?" he asks glancing sideways away from the road.

"Everything. Dealing with new people, the prophecy, being me." I sigh, not knowing how to articulate what I'm feeling.

"It'll all work out, Princess." Vance grins, trying to make me feel better.

We pull up in the parking lot, which is slowly filling up. I take a deep breath before climbing out of the truck. As I help lift my bags from the bed of his truck, I straighten my back in resolve. I will be confident and not let anyone see fear. This thought makes my panther sit up straighter and prouder, over the last week we've connected more and more.

I make my way to my dorm room, leaving Vance behind to wait for the guys, wanting to get stuff put away as soon as possible.

As I pass the noble floor, I hear Amy making snarky comments.

"Oh look, it's the new royal who thinks she has a chance with any of those guys. Maybe she's a slut and sleeping with them all," she tells Kelly loudly so I can overhear.

Kylah gets upset but I ignore her and keep moving, upsetting her even further. I run up the rest of the stairs and drop my bags as soon as I open my door.

"We should teach them a lesson. We are not weak, and they are horrid," Kylah growls, reverberating in my throat.

"We can't, that will get us in trouble, please calm down," I beg.

"We need to let them know we are better than them," she roars.

I grab my phone and text.

Me: 911

Kenton: What's wrong?

Me: Mean girls upset Kylah, and I can't calm her down in my room.

Kenton: Coming.

I pace back and forth trying to match her movements hoping to calm her down. Seconds later, there's a knock on the door. I open it and the lion shifter comes in and grabs me in a big hug instantly calming Kylah. I can feel her purring in my chest.

"I didn't expect that to work but was hoping it would," Kenton whispers in my ear.

I can feel his chest vibrating against mine, so his lion must be just as content. I relax into him.

"He's mine. My mate," she purrs, melting into him further.

"Yes, mate," Percy purrs back.

"Our cats are at home," he whispers his forehead against mine.

"I'm not ready to date anyone in the group. I meant it when I said that before," I reply, Kylah sulking. A part of me is over the moon by the announcement, but I don't want to lose any of the guys. They are the first group that made it feel okay to be here, and I just can't jeopardize that.

"Doesn't change facts," he says then kisses my forehead and lets me go.

He quietly leaves the room, making my heart break just a little. Why can't I just have all of them? I think to myself, causing my panther to perk up and start purring.

"Oh no you don't," I tell her aloud. She just huffs and lays down in the back of my mind again.

I busy myself putting everything away and decorating the room, which seems less empty with the new furniture Jack ordered. An hour later, things are feeling much more put together and like home. I decide to text the group, hoping Kenton isn't mad at me.

Me: I'm finally organized, how are you guys?

Dom: Hanging out in Kenton's, come over.

Kenton: Only if you can stand our company.

Spence: WTF is your problem?

Me: I guess I'll stay here since Kenton doesn't want me around.

I toss the phone down and cry, and I mean ugly cry. I don't want to lose my group but pushing him away might have had the same effect. Seconds later, there are fists pounding on my door.

"Killer, open up this door now," Spence booms, his voice full of worry and anger.

I wipe my eyes as I stand to answer the door to four angry faces and a fifth that refuses to raise their eyes from the ground. My red face and swollen eyes are the first thing to greet them.

"Why are you crying?" Dom demands, the muscle in his jaw ticking.

"What happened between the two of you?" Reid asks confused.

"I'm crying because it hurt when Kenton didn't want me to come over and he can tell you the rest," I whisper, trying to hold back my tears.

"Fine, our cats said we're mates, and she rejected me, so I'm pissed. She said she doesn't want to ruin our friendship," he snarls then stomps away, causing me to break fully into sobs.

Spence rushes forward and scoops me in his arms holding me tight, causing my heartache to ease a bit.

"He's mine too. My mate," Kylah purrs, content as can be.

"Not again, I will lose all of you because I can't choose any of you, aren't I?" I scream, sobbing harder.

I feel more sets of arms surrounding me and my cat responds the same to each.

"We have five mates; we'll be well taken care of," Kylah purrs so loud I can feel my chest vibrating.

"How can I be so defective that my cat wants me to be

with all of you?" I crumble to the ground going limp between their arms.

"I will go get Kenton; we need to have a talk and explain cat culture to Jet," Reid explains then leaves the room.

I wipe my eyes and ask, "What do you mean?"

"Wait until Reid and Kenton come back. He needs to eat some crow after the way he treated you, Kitten." Dom rubs circles on my back.

A few minutes later, Reid is back with a sulking Kenton following him. I feel like pulling myself inwardly when I see him. My heart hurts, and I want to run and hug him; my panther agrees, but I refuse.

"Now that we're all back, Jet, I'm guessing where you came from is monogamous?" Reid asks.

"Yes, like most of the world," I reply, confused on where this is going.

"In cat society, our females usually have two to five mates. When we're sixteen and older our cats tell us who we're meant to be with if we meet them. When you tried to tell Kenton that you didn't want to date him because of the group, he thought you were rejecting him because you were hoping for a different mate," Reid explains, holding my hand gently.

"I wasn't rejecting you," I say peering up at Kenton, "I was afraid if I were with one of you, it could ruin your friendship if something went wrong."

Kenton's face suddenly brightens with understanding, and he rushes forward and scoops me up off the floor holding me tight. He kisses me forehead and says, "I knew you were trouble."

"You don't hate me?" I ask, afraid to let my guard down.

"We will always love you, even when you don't us," Percy says.

"How could I hate you? It hurt that you didn't want me,

and I handled it wrong. I've forgotten you haven't always been with us," he explains, his features dropping in sorrow.

"So, it really doesn't bother any of you that Kylah wants to be with all of you?" I ask, nervously, scared that they wouldn't want to be with me.

"Of course not! We've always been brothers; this means we'll always be together regardless of class. We'll all be royal eventually now," Dom says then kisses my forehead.

"Put the princess down so I can hug her," Vance says coming up behind me.

Kenton complies and Vance spins me around in a bone-crushing hug. I finally feel content and whole though I'm scared at the thought of dating five guys at once.

"Nothing has to change between us right now, Trouble. Just knowing what we're meant for is enough for me," Kenton explains, picking up on my anxiety.

"That helps a lot," I answer pulling out of Vance's embrace finding Spence ready to hug me again. "Though it looks like I'll have to get used to lots of hugs."

"Sorry, Tress wants to be close to you." Spence gives me a sheepish grin but holds me tighter his chest vibrating with his tiger's purr.

"I feel the same way about all of you; it's overwhelming," I admit as Spence releases me. "I'm not ready to be in a public relationship with five guys outside of friendship."

"I'm down with that," Dom smirks.

"I'm happy with whatever makes you happy, Princess," Vance speaks up.

"It's agreed. We'll stay friends in public with Trouble," Kenton says, grabbing my hand, "But in private, Percy won't be happy unless we can touch you."

"I can deal with that." I never imagined how much my life could change in a matter of weeks, yet here I am standing in a group of boys that would protect me and do anything for me. Maybe life at Nightfall won't be so bad.

"What time do we have to be at the auditorium?" I ask, remembering there's an assembly before lunch.

"Um, now. Let's go," Reid answers glancing at his phone screen.

We take off out of my room and down the stairs. As we pass by the second floor, Amy and Kelly are still standing around.

"See, total slut," Amy says loudly making Kylah come running towards the surface.

"Oh, and how many mates are you hoping to have?" Dom snarks at her, his hackles raised.

"Well, I um, don't talk to me commoner," she stammers and turns beet red.

Kylah stops in her tracks with her mate's defense of her. I give him a smile of relief and we continue on our way to assembly.

I'm not looking forward to the seating in the assembly. The rules are archaic. Genders are separated, and we're also separated by class. Royals sit up front, nobles in the middle, and commoners in the back. I wish this system didn't leave me on my own but glad it keeps me away from Amy, Kelly, and Krissy.

Once in the auditorium, Kenton and I walk to the front together me branching to the left and him to the right once we hit the first row. We have assigned seats that correspond with our room numbers; I roll my eyes at how planned out this is. A blonde girl sits further down the row, but she ignores me, so I just stare at the front stage until a tall redheaded girl with emerald green eyes sits next to me.

"Hi! I'm Rachael, second year here," she introduces herself.

"Lia, and my first, obviously," I chuckle nervously.

"It's not so bad once you learn your way around; assembly is the only place they seat us like this. I'd rather be over there next to that fine lion, Kenton," she chatters while ogling him.

Kylah growls before I can choke it back.

"Sorry, I didn't know anyone had claimed him already. How long ago, was it romantic? How long have you known each other?" she rattles off questions.

"I met him a week ago, it scared me more than was romantic, and it happened about an hour ago," I told her truthfully. Something makes me want to trust her.

"You're so lucky, but you will have a sign on your back now. Good thing you're royal or you would have some issues," she says, twirling a lock of her crimson hair.

"Great, what I need is more drama," I sigh and sit back.

"Just wait, you have to answer when Sir asks if we have made any mates," she whispers the auditorium growing quiet.

"That's a thing?" I hiss back scared to death.

"Yeah, all mating bonds have to be registered. The good news is you'll get to sit with Kenton in the mated section after this," she tries to comfort me.

"What if I had multiple mates show themselves today, in theory?" I ask, my palms sweating, feeling an uncontrolled shift coming.

"Then you are one lucky girl! Is it all of Kenton's group? That would be my dream right there!" she exclaims guessing straight away. The expression my face says it all. "Truthfully, that is the best thing that could have happened for them. They would have been separated after school otherwise."

"I wasn't ready to go public with this yet," I whisper my anxiety making my entire body vibrate.

Kenton glances over and sees the state I'm in and rushes over and holds my hands. If I didn't have to out us anyway, this would have done the trick.

"What's wrong, Trouble?" Kenton asks, I can feel the worry coming off him in waves.

"We have to announce our mates today in assembly," I whisper; my panther calming down with him near.

"Sorry, Trouble," he whispers then rushes back to his seat.

"Don't worry, it's not a big deal. They'll call your cats forward, test the bond then let you guys go. I've seen it loads of times. I can't wait until I find mine," she sighs; her eyes glossing over in a daydream.

My cat sniffs the air then purrs. Suddenly Rachael's eyes get big, and she wraps me in a big hug.

"She's our sister," Kylah announces proudly.

"I'm Kaila, nice to meet you," Rachael's leopard says.

"I always hoped I would have a chosen family!" she exclaims tears falling from her eyes.

"Welcome to mine, sister," I say unsure of what else to say.

"We have to announce this too. My leopard is so happy right now she's purring through my chest!" she squeals, her hands fidgeting with her hair.

Sir steps up to the podium on stage, and the room gets so quiet, I can hear myself breathing. He starts a speech about welcoming us to the new semester, and I zone out until Rachael elbows me in the ribs.

"... any new mating bonds since our last assembly?" I catch the end of his question.

My five guys and I stand up.

"Come forward and state who you have bonded with please," Sir orders, and we comply joining him on the stage.

"Amelia Huntsman, do you have any bonds which you would like to claim?" he asks, his face an unreadable mask.

"Yes, Sir, Vance Avery, Dominic Perrie, Spencer Williams, Reid Thielman, and Kenton Huntsman," I answer, my voice warbling.

The crowd gasps and chatter breaks out loudly.

"Silence!" Sir booms from the podium. "Remove your clothes and shift now!"

We do as he says, undress, and I slip into my panther faster than I've ever shifted before. A man comes out on stage and does a quick chant that I can't understand, and a shimmering black cord made from the magic wraps around each of the guys, heading to me. There's also a green cord that wraps around each of the guys to each other, a separate one leading from me to Rachael, and one that leads out the building, I'm guessing to Jack.

The cords disappear, and I shift back and put my clothes back on. The guys are doing the same once I'm dressed.

"Amelia Huntsman, you are making many bonds very young, I think we can expect great things from you," Sir says, dismissing us off the stage.

"Rachael Huntsman, we acknowledge your family bond with Amelia and grant you permission to sit with your family if you would like," Sir says.

He doesn't finish talking before she's out of her seat running towards us sitting in the section to the far left of the stage for mates.

"Isn't it wonderful?! Your family is already built, and you don't have to worry about wondering when it will happen." She hugs me, vibrating with excitement.

he assembly finally finishes, and we take the stairs to the cafeteria. I want to eat quickly and call Jack. I hear Kylah calling to him.

"Leave him alone," I chastise.

"We need all our family," she says as if it's obvious.

"If you don't get your panther under control, Jack will be up here soon," Kenton whispers in my ear.

"You can hear that too?" I ask amazed.

"We all can honey. Who's Jack, her other family bond?" Rachael asks between bites of food.

"I found out he was my brother a few days after meeting him," I reply, still wanting to see him badly.

Kylah perks up, and I can tell he's close suddenly. I turn around and can see Jace coming down the stairs, huffing through his mouth like he's smelling for something. I get up out of my chair and run to him and wrap my arms around his neck.

I let go, and he shifts back human, one of the cafeteria workers handing him a robe.

"What's wrong little sister? We couldn't ignore your call," he asks, his forehead wrinkled in worry.

"I'm sorry. We had to announce our mates today and family bonds, and I guess it upset my panther you weren't here when that happened." I stare at the ground embarrassed that he ran all the way here for that.

"I think I need more information." Jack's eyes dart around the group but when his eyes land on Rachael his face lights up and I can almost see the bond forming before my eyes.

They rush forward, each of them forgetting their surroundings, as if they are the only ones to exist in their worlds. When the reach each other, they lock in an embrace that makes me uncomfortable to watch, then he leans over and kisses her. I guess she got the romantic bond she was hoping for, with my brother. It clicks… That's why she's my sister.

My heart fills with joy with the fact that they found each other. I turn to sit back down, and Kenton is behind me, so I lean back on him. My panther content now that her family is complete.

Jack pulls back from Rachael suddenly and swivels around, his cheeks turning bright red. "Sorry about that, Lia. Let's eat and talk."

"It's ok. Kylah is happy now that you're here with my new sister Rachael, you know the girl you kissed without asking her name," I tease him, watching his face grow a brighter shade of crimson.

"Sorry, I'm Jack, nice to meet you Rachael," he kneels on the ground kissing her hand.

"So romantic," she gushes, then gives me a hug.

"Ok, some girls upset me then Kenton came over and my panther said he was my mate. I made him mad, the rest of the guys came over, and my panther decided they were all my mates too. I sat down next to Rachael then found out she's my sister, then Sir called for bonds at the assembly. I had to shift in front of the whole school, then my panther started screaming for you," I explain in one breath, rushing to get all the words out.

"That's a lot to handle in one day! Are you ok?" he asks his face lined with concern.

"I'm good. I didn't think I wanted the news out, but now that it is, my panther is happier," I explain. "At least now, everyone knows they are officially off limits, and Amy's slut comments are unfounded."

"She called you a slut for hanging out with these guys?" Rachael's face darkens and her brow turns down.

She gets up and stomps over to the table Amy is sitting at and I can see the girl go pale as a sheet.

"If I ever hear that you say anything at all about my sister, I will grind you into the ground you worthless noble. Do you understand?" Rachael growls at her and you can almost see the steam coming out of her ears.

"I...," Amy cannot say anything. Her eyes grow wide and her mouth continually opens and closes silently like a fish on land.

Rachael walks back over to our table smiling and sits next to Jack. "She's feared me since we were little. She called my doll ugly, so I kicked her in the face."

"Thank you for standing up for me. I feel so blessed to have found this awesome of a family," I say, meaning every word.

We finish eating lunch then Jack and Rachael return to her room to get to know each other better. The guys and I go our separate ways. I'm emotionally exhausted and want a nap so I can be ready for whatever the evening assembly holds for us. I'm feeling like I might just love my time at Nightfall.

EPILOGUE

"That's right. A panther princess who's bonded to five males," the unknown man whispers on the phone from the corner of the empty auditorium.

"All known princesses were exterminated. Where did she come from?" the voice on the other line asks.

"I know we thought all the panthers in the royal line had been taken care of too," he replies to the line.

"What do you plan to do about this? We can't have the prophecy come true," the voice hisses.

"I'll monitor her, but we might have to take her out if she appears too powerful," he says, rubbing his fingers together anxiously.

"You won't have to get your hands dirty. Call us and we will take care of your black kitten for you," the voice says then hangs up.

To be continued...

. . .

READY FOR THE next installment of The Huntsman Clan? Check out Royal.

ACKNOWLEDGMENTS

Thank you to my husband for putting up with all my time spent in front of the computer working on this book.

Thank you to my kids for pushing me to write something they could read.

Thank you to all my author friends for your support.

Pike, you are the glue, this wouldn't have happened without your help so thank you bunches.

ABOUT THE AUTHOR

Rose lives in the Midwest with her husband, kids and three cats. She enjoys crafting in her free time and watching movies with her family.

Sign up for our Newsletter get a free story
Rose Alexander Author Page
Rose's Reverie - Readers Group
Rose Alexander - Instagram
Rose Alexander Twitter
Rose Alexander Pinterest
Academy of Broken Dreams Reader's Group (Co-writes)